The G W9-CVA-867

THE GHOST
OF FIVE OWL
FARM

By the same author

THE GHOST
OF FIVE OWL
FARM

Wilson Gage, *pseud.*

Steele, Mary Q

J
STE

Illustrated by Paul Galdone

COLLINS 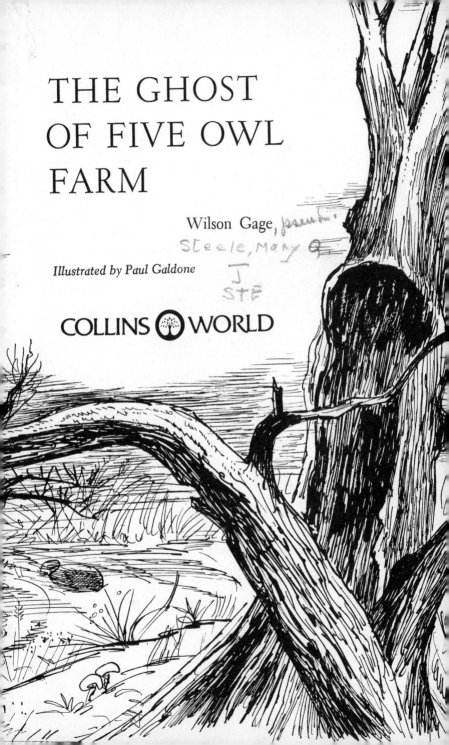 WORLD

*For Peggy Beals, with thanks for those
buttons in those hot dogs—and with love.*

Published by William Collins + World Publishing Company
2080 West 117th Street
Cleveland, Ohio 44111

Published simultaneously in Canada by
Nelson, Foster & Scott Ltd.

Library of Congress Cataloging in Publication Data

Steele, Mary Q
  The ghost of Five Owl Farm.

  SUMMARY: When his twin cousins come to visit, Ted
decides to frighten them with ghost stories. Then to his
surprise, he discovers something spooky really is going on
in the barn.
  [1. Ghost stories] I. Galdone, Paul. II. Title.
PZ7.S8146Gh4   [Fic]   75-20088
ISBN 0-529-03889-7 lib. bdg.

◈ Chapter One

It was nearly a mile from the point where Ted Garland got off the bus to his house. That was one of the few things Ted had disliked about moving into the new place. At least he had thought he would dislike it. Actually it had turned out to be one of the really great things about the farm. The very first day he walked that mile it was cold and windy; halfway home snow had begun to fall. He had been lost in a blizzard, stumbling along knowing that he *must* get the mail through. Or no: it was serum—serum for the children of the Indian village exposed to some dreadful disease.

Long after his faithful pony had fallen victim to the storm, he had staggered on, muttering between clenched teeth, "I must make it. Lives are depending on me. I *must* get through." He had arrived home half frozen and wholly happy, and since then he had looked forward to his walk with anticipation.

A few days after the "blizzard," he had come upon a beautiful quartz arrowhead lying in the middle of

the little muddy road, uncovered by the torrential
rains of early spring. And not long after that he had
found a mysterious machine under a bush near the
road, where people had been dumping for years. It
turned out to be the innards of an old-fashioned
phonograph, and Ted had a lot of fun with it.

For a week during March he had walked with his
face turned up to the sky—and his knees bruised and
his blue jeans muddy from frequent falls—to see the
flights of geese and ducks going north along the river.
Ted had never seen anything like it in his life, the

sky filled with streams of birds, the air alive with the sound of their wings and the deep lovely voices of the geese. It made his heart race and his skin prickle just to remember it.

This afternoon there were no geese, but there were lots of other birds. Flocks of sparrows and juncos flew up out of the road as he walked along, and over there in the haw bushes, just beginning to be sprinkled with white blossoms, he heard a queer song that he'd heard frequently the past week. "Chick-a-per-wee-oo-chick!" cried the bird over and over, and it struck Ted as a pretty dumb thing to say. Nevertheless the bird said it often and said it emphatically. It reminded Ted of Mrs. Bryant, the music teacher at school, and the way she said "Pay attention to the time!" over and over when the class was singing. Ted thought that made about as much sense as "Chick-a-per-wee-oo-chick!" His time sense wasn't very good.

He stopped and stood still to see if he could get a glimpse of the bird. After a minute something stirred in the underbrush. Something was coming out.

But it wasn't a bird. Ted almost yelled with surprise when he saw it. It was a fox, a little red plumy-tailed fox with a sharp black nose and sharp pale ears. Ted had never seen a live fox before in his whole life. He certainly hadn't known there were any living this close to his house. It startled him so he couldn't do a thing except stand there absolutely still.

The fox paused and turned her thin, pretty little head and stared straight at him, but he was so still she must have thought he was some new kind of tree or scarecrow or something. She paid no attention to him. She chewed at a flea on her foreleg, looked off across the fields, and then trotted up the muddy road.

Ted watched. He had had no idea a living creature could be that weightless. She ran so lightly it was as if the earth pushed up on her slim little feet at each step and sent her bouncing along. She disappeared around a bend in the road and Ted ran after her. But when he rounded the curve, she was gone.

He stood there with his tennis shoes covered with mud and grinned to himself. He'd find that fox and watch her again, he knew he would. Maybe she had a den with little ones somewhere near. Off to his right he could hear frogs calling from the low place in the field where pools of rain water collected. He'd tried a thousand times to sneak up on them. But no matter how quietly he went, they heard him and disappeared long before he reached the edge of the water.

He cut across a field where bird's-foot violets sprang up in little clumps like blue pincushions underfoot. Pink and white spring beauties sprawled among them, and chickweed and dandelions. One of the neighboring farmers grazed his herd in this field. Ted had seen cows here only last week. He wondered if cows ate bird's-foot violets and if they tasted better than clover.

Daddy was home, his car was in the driveway. Ted hadn't known he would be home early today. He clumped around on the front steps, trying to get the mud off his sneakers, and finally decided the thing to do was to take them off and leave them on the porch.

Sock-footed, he opened the door and went in. Mr. Garland was at his desk on the little glassed-in porch which overlooked the river. Ted shuffled out to see him.

"Hello," he began. His father jumped and spilled some papers on the floor.

"For the love of mud," he said. "Don't sneak up on me that way. I'm already jumpy enough living in a haunted house."

Ted sat down in an old leather chair, getting into it the way he liked to get into chairs if nobody stopped him, swinging his legs over the back and sliding down into the seat. "Is this really a haunted house, Daddy?" he asked. "A lot of the kids at school say it is. Bob Fentress said his dad spent the night in the old barn once, and he saw lights and heard rattles and bangs all night long."

His father stooped to pick up his papers but Ted could see he was grinning to himself. "Sure, it's haunted," he said. "The basement is haunted by spiders, the pantry by mice, and the attic by squirrels. And we haunt the rest of it. That's what haunt means, you know, to live in or frequent. You can look it up in the dictionary if you don't believe me."

"I believe you," Ted answered, spreading his knees wide and trying to get the soles of his feet flat together. His father was a newspaperman, and one thing he knew about was words. "Anyway, you knew I was only kidding. I gave up believing in ghosts a long time ago. I just meant do you suppose there was anything around here that might make people *think* there were ghosts, like—like—you know—like—"

"Like foxfire, St. Elmo's fire, or will-o'-the-wisps," finished Mr. Garland. "Or a flaw in the earth which carries sounds over great distances or a hidden deposit of radioactive material or something. Not that I know of. What Bob Fentress's father saw was either the product of his own imagination or some playful little arrangement cooked up by his friends."

"I guess so," agreed Ted. "It's just that Five Owl Farm sounds like a good place for a ghost, for one thing. And then the Indians—well, Indians make pretty good ghosts, I guess."

Mr. Garland nodded. "Yes, if anybody really had a reason to come back from the dead, it must be Chief Five Owl," he said thoughtfully. "This beautiful farm, here in the land of the Cherokees, his house and all his meadows and fields and his barns stuffed with corn —all of it snatched from him overnight by the white people for their own selfish ends. And then to be sent away into the flat dusty lands of the West. It killed him, you know. He died on the journey, though he was still a youngish man."

Ted chewed a thumb meditatively. It was an awful thing; he sort of wished he'd never heard the story. Still the farm was certainly a happy place now. He'd lived in three different houses before this and none had been half so nice or anywhere near as much fun.

Suddenly Ted lifted his head. Did he smell cookies? Was his mother baking cookies? He and Mr. Garland exchanged glances. "I don't know," said his father. "I haven't tasted one yet."

Ted sniffed again. "They *smell* all right," he said worriedly.

"That doesn't mean a thing," his father pointed out. "So did the ones she used fish food in instead of nutmeg."

Ted's mother was a good cook. When she made a successful pie or cake, it was a mouth-watering pie or cake. The only trouble was, somehow being out in the kitchen made her absent-minded. She was a great gardener—it was one of the reasons they had moved to the farm, so she could have more space for flowers—and once she started gardening in her imagination, she was apt to cook without really paying attention to what she was doing. She might use liquid cleaner instead of cooking oil, she might leave out vital ingredients or put them in two or three times over, and more than once she had put a sheet of cookies in the refrigerator to bake.

Every time she was terribly upset she would wring her hands and cry, "Oh, what a waste, how could I have been so stupid!" and each time she would resolve to do better. When they first moved to the farm, she had done so many absent-minded things that now she cooked with all the kitchen shades drawn down to the sill.

"If I once look out the window," she explained, "I

start moving lilac bushes and planting day lilies, and then goodness knows what happens. But if I can't see the lilac bushes, it's easier for me to concentrate on cooking."

Now Ted struggled up out of his chair. "I'll take a chance," he said, grinning. He picked up his jacket and books and started out of the room. "Oh, I saw a fox on my way home, a real live one. It was neat. When it ran, it was . . ." He stopped, remembering that bubble-light step and the grace of the small furry body. "It was neat," he ended finally.

"I'm not surprised," his father said, turning back to his papers. "There are probably a good many wild things around here. Keep your eyes open. There were deer tracks all over the place when I was out here last winter."

Deer tracks! Ted stumped up the steps to the second floor. Oh, boy, he hoped the deer were still around. He guessed he must be the luckiest boy in the whole fifty states. The minute he'd laid eyes on the farm, on the big white house sitting in the middle of a meadow grown up to young sassafras trees and blackberry bushes, he'd known this was the place he wanted to live in more than any other place in the world. The land around the house sloped down to the Tennessee River on one side and on the other stretched away in a series of small rolling knolls and valleys to the mountains.

Ted went to the window of his low-ceilinged white painted room and stared off toward those hills, tender blue, with the hollows shaded lavender, "the color of heartbreak," his mother had said. "Chief Five Owl's heartbreak, not mine," thought Ted unfeelingly.

He didn't really mean to be callous. It was just that it was spring, the start of a ten-day vacation from school, and he was living here in this place where foxes and deer lived, where once the Cherokee braves had come to visit a chief, and long before that another race of Indians had built mounds of mussel shells and left their broken pottery to turn up wherever his mother lifted the earth to plant a daffodil bulb.

From his window Ted couldn't see the river. He could see the front lawn, which gradually blurred into the surrounding fields. The fields were split by the winding muddy track that Ted followed on his way to and from the bus, and that the Garlands' car followed after it left the highway. Ted's sister, Rosemary, called it a "private road," but the truth was it was hardly more than a rutted trail.

A hundred yards or so from the house a second trail branched off from this main one. It had been unused so long it was barely visible. It meandered up a hill till it ended under a vast oak tree, right outside the old barn. The barn hadn't had a cow in it for thirty years, Daddy said. A little grove of hackberry trees had grown up along one side and an ancient orchard grew on the other, so in summer the building was almost invisible from the house. But now the tiny ferny leaves of the hackberry and the swinging yellow tassels of the oak did very little to hide it.

In the orchard the peach blossoms had come and gone, but apples and pears were still blooming. Scattered among the twisted trunks was some bedraggled farm machinery, including a tractor which Ted felt sure could be made to run again if he could scrape off about a ton of rust so he could see what was wrong.

Steven Miller, Ted's best friend, lived close enough so that half an hour's bicycling, with only one hill so steep that you had to dismount and push, brought them together. Ted grinned. He could hardly wait. Between school and bad weather he really hadn't had a chance to explore the Garlands' six acres. Day after tomorrow Steve would come over to stay the next four days, and Ted meant to leave no stone unturned, from the rickety little fishing pier on the muddy river bank to the last stand of poplar and maple against the farthest fence.

He got another pair of shoes out of the closet. Through the wall he could hear the murmur of his sister's voice. She was singing. He had to admit that having Rosemary go to visit her best friend, Sally Beston, for a few days wasn't exactly going to make him break down and cry. Rosemary was as good as the next sister, he supposed. Anyway, she wasn't fat or stupid or anything. Still, having the whole place to himself was a thing he enjoyed once in a while, and now was an ideal time to enjoy it.

He clumped down the steps and out into the kitchen. His mother was taking a pan of cookies out of the oven, and a plate filled with them was on the table. The shades were pulled right down to the sills.

Ted took a cookie from the plate. He turned it over and over and inspected it carefully. Then he broke off the tiniest little crumb to taste. His mother stamped her foot. "Now stop that!" she cried. "They're perfectly all right. I just ate one myself."

Ted judiciously chewed a mouthful. "Well, they taste all right," he admitted. "You sure you didn't put something tasteless in them, some bug spray that will poison us all slowly?"

"Well, I'm not sure," admitted Mrs. Garland. "But if I have I'll be the first to suffer the ill effects. I've eaten three already, to say nothing of some raw dough. Would you like some milk?"

Ted got a glass of milk and sat down once again, chewing his cooky and watching his mother put another pan in the oven and flour the pastry board to roll out some more dough. There seemed to be a lot of dough. He had a sudden agonizing suspicion.

"Why are you making such a lot of cookies?" he asked sharply. "There's enough there for two families already."

His mother glanced at him apologetically. "Well, I guess you might as well know," she said. "Uncle Matt and Aunt Julie—"

Ted fell off his stool with a howl. "Oh, no!" he wailed. "Not the twins! Oh, no!"

✒ Chapter Two

"Roll up your window, Ted," cried Rosemary passionately. "The wind is blowing my hair all to bits!"

"Come on, Ted, roll it up," Mr. Garland said. "She'll be getting out in another mile. Then you can roll it down. I don't mind a little wind."

Silently Ted wound the window up tight. He supposed when the twins got in they'd have to seal the windows shut. The twins were so little and skinny a draft might not just muss their hair; it might scatter the twins themselves up among the treetops. Oh, why did Uncle Matt and Aunt Julie have to pick this week to decide to go to Jamaica and send their children to stay with the Garlands?

Mr. Garland glanced in the mirror at Rosemary sitting in the back seat. "What are you and Sally going to do all this time?" he asked. "Won't you get tired of each other?"

"Oh, no," answered Rosemary. "We never get tired of each other. And there's plenty to do. We're going to a party at Jean Henderson's. And Mrs. Beston is going to take us to town for lunch. And we can talk on the telephone."

"Oh, boy," agreed Ted. "You can do that, all right. You two are experts. You've had enough practice."

Rosemary glared. "And we're going to do something new with Sally's hair," she went on, talking to the back of her father's neck and ignoring Ted. "And Mrs. Beston is going to teach us to knit. And she knows a game called Botticelli for Two Heads. Sally says it's fun and we can play it lots."

"Well," exclaimed Mr. Garland. "Here we are and I guess it's a good thing. With a program like that ahead of you, you'd better get started right away."

Ted watched while his father helped Rosemary carry her various boxes and suitcases up to the door. He supposed he should have offered to carry something. But Rosemary always objected to the way he did things, so he'd gotten to where he just never stuck his neck out.

Besides he had an ordeal ahead of him and he might as well save his strength. A whole six days of the twins! He didn't think he could bear it. The night before, he had felt fairly hopeful. Something would save him. Something would happen to Jamaica before Aunt Julie and Uncle Matt got there. It would be blown away by a storm, or repealed, or something. They would have to come home and look after their own children.

Now, however, as he and his father drove along toward the bus station, he knew it was useless to hope.

His spring vacation was going to be overrun by twins. He wouldn't even be able to have Steve over because there wasn't any point in inflicting the twins on Steve. Do as you would be done to, was the way Ted figured it. If the twins had been Steve's cousins, Ted would have preferred not being with them.

He and his father rode in silence for a while. Finally Mr. Garland said, "It's that bad, huh?"

"Worse," Ted answered. He reflected. "I wish it hadn't been so sudden. I had a lot of plans. And then Mother just up and let me have it, right between the eyes. If I had three eyes, I guess you'd have to say she let me have it right *among* the eyes," he added glumly. Miss Prentice, his sixth grade teacher, was always after him about the proper use of "between" and "among."

"The twins are different and kind of odd, but I like them," Mr. Garland said. "What is it you find so hard to bear?"

"They're just awful!" Ted burst out. "Winkie and Bobbin, for Pete's sake! Why can't they be called by their real names, Cynthia and Robert, or Bob, like—like human beings! And they don't have any sense, Daddy, you know they don't. Bottlecelli for Two Heads would be a good game for them, Daddy. They've got two heads all right, but they've only got one brain between them."

"Botticelli," corrected his father absently. "I can't really think of anything so awfully stupid they've done."

"Maybe you can't, but I can," muttered Ted. That

Bobbin, Ted reflected, didn't know anything about anything. He couldn't play baseball or even softball. He didn't know a piston ring from an apple. And when the twins rode bicycles, they wobbled.

"Well, Daddy, you remember about the clothes drier," Ted said at last.

Mr. Garland chuckled. "That was pretty dumb," he admitted.

You'd expect the twins to be too dumb to come in out of the rain, thought Ted. And you'd expect them to be dumb enough to think they could dry their clothes in an electric drier while they were still wearing them. What you might not have expected was that they would both get into the drier at the same time. They had gotten stuck, so that before Aunt Julie had had a chance to use her new drier even once, a repairman had to come and take it all apart and prize the twins out of it.

Maybe you couldn't blame the twins. Maybe they just didn't know *how* to think. But it was certain the next few days were going to be no vacation for Ted.

The bus was just pulling into the station when Ted and his father parked in the parking lot. The twins were the very last passengers off. Ted had not dared to hope they had improved in the six months since he had last seen them, and sure enough they hadn't. They were still as skinny and white-faced as ever. Dressed exactly alike in blue jeans and white shirts and brown jackets, they were practically indistinguishable, especially with Winkie's hair cut very short due to her notion that coating it with airplane glue would make it curl. They looked much younger than their ten years. Their pale faces, light blue eyes, and tow-colored hair always made Ted think they were so close to invisible they were going to disappear altogether in just a second or two, but he despaired of its ever really happening.

Bobbin consulted his watch. "It took three hours and twenty-six minutes," he announced. He liked to know everything very exactly.

"You took half that time getting off the bus," grumbled Ted. "What were you doing?"

"We were looking for Freddy," explained Bobbin.

"Freddy got lost," Winkie added.

Daddy looked alarmed. "Did you find him?" he asked. "Where is he?"

Silently Winkie held out her hand. There, curled in her palm, was a small chameleon, dry and dusty.

Daddy poked him. "I'm afraid Freddy's dead," he said gently.

"I suppose so," said Winkie and sighed. "He hasn't moved for two days now. I didn't want to leave him at home for fear he should revive all by himself and there'd be nobody to give him food and water."

Ted couldn't help being interested in the chameleon. "Did he use to change color?" he asked.

Bobbin shook his head. "He never did. Daddy said he was defective. That's how he got his name, Freddy the Defective."

Mr. Garland grinned and Ted snorted. "That was a

long time ago," said Winkie with dignity. "We know now it's Freddy the Detective."

"There're your bags," said Mr. Garland. "Come along. Lunch will be waiting at the farm."

And so it was. The kind of lunch Ted liked best, bacon and tomato sandwiches and cocoa with marshmallows *and* whipped cream. He guessed it wasn't his mother's fault that she didn't remember what huge appetites the twins had in spite of their anemic appearance. By using the very last little crumbs of bacon and some rather lopsided slices of tomato, Ted managed to scrape together a second sandwich for himself. The twins had each had three and were now contentedly finishing up the cocoa.

"Don't you two think you'd better go upstairs and lie down after lunch?" asked Mrs. Garland. Ted gloated. He might have known Mother would rescue him.

The twins looked surprised. "Why should we lie down?" asked Bobbin.

"To rest after your trip," Mrs. Garland said.

"We don't need to rest; it wasn't hard," explained Winkie. "We just sat there. We didn't do a thing to get tired."

Mrs. Garland laughed. "I guess not," she said and gave Ted a sympathetic look. "Well, run along then. If you're going out, wear your jackets. The sun's warm, but the wind off the river is chilly still."

Ted fetched his own jacket and went gloomily out of doors. It was a perfect afternoon. The sky was like blue velvet and the sun was hot on his bare head, but the air was fresh and cool. The trees were fogged over with a haze of little new greeny-gold leaves, and here and there the dogwoods spread their white branches.

On the porch behind him the twins hopped and chirped like a couple of nutty baby birds. Ted eased away along the path toward the barn. He wasn't going to lose his dignity by sneaking away from them, but if they didn't bother to notice he was leaving, it wasn't his fault.

He made it to the barn undiscovered. He went around on the other side of the big weather-beaten building and there under the branches of the gnarled old fruit trees stood the broken-down tractor. Ted looked at it with admiring eyes. Daddy had tried to convince him that vital pieces of its insides were missing, but Ted was sure he could get the thing running again if he just had the proper tools and enough time. It might not run well, but it would run.

He bent over the engine and began to poke at various wheels and springs. He had put vinegar on a few of the screws a couple of days ago, and now he rubbed at them with his handkerchief to see if the rust was dissolving. He took a screwdriver from his pocket and began to work.

By and by he straightened his aching back and took off his jacket. Here, sheltered from the wind, it was really hot. The smell of apple blossoms filled the air. A lot of bees growled at each other among the branches. He could see the pollen baskets on their legs bulging with creamy powder as they bumped in and out among the white flowers and the shining green leaves. And beyond the bees and the clusters of blossoms and the pattern of old black branches was that deep, caressing, cloudless sky.

Ted turned back to the tractor—and there was Bobbin halfway inside the thing. For these few happy minutes Ted had forgotten all about the twins, so it was a double shock. "What are you doing here?" he asked angrily.

"I'm looking," answered Bobbin calmly. "There's a mud dauber's nest in here."

And so there was, two long columns of mud plastered close to the metal. Ted hadn't noticed it before. "It's nearly the same color as the rust," he told himself. "And anyway I wasn't looking for mud daubers' nests or I would have seen them long ago."

"It'll never run," announced Bobbin a minute later.

"It will too," Ted declared hotly. "Where's Cynthia? Why don't you go find her?"

"She's down by the river," said Bobbin. "I expect she'll fall in."

Somebody screamed. Over the gentle sounds of wind and bees a shrill voice shrieked over and over, "Oh, help, help, help, help!"

"There," said Bobbin in the satisfied voice of one who has had a prediction come true. "She's done it already."

Ted ran. He could swim and he'd had a life-saving course last summer. But could he really rescue someone who was drowning? He hoped to goodness Daddy had heard the screams. "Help, Daddy, help!" he bawled as he sped past the house.

There was Winkie. But she wasn't in the river. She was crouched in a little heap on the fishing dock and was still screeching steadily. What in the world? Ted wondered. Snake bite? Sprained ankle? Earthquake? What could make anybody yell like that?

Mr. Garland rushed by him and seized Winkie by the shoulders. "Winkie, what's the matter?" he cried. His face was white, but Winkie's when she raised it was red with tears and exertion.

"Oh, help," she sobbed. "What am I going to do with this old *thing*?"

She looked down at her hands. A piece of string was wrapped around and around them, cutting deep into what little flesh she possessed. The string disappeared between two boards of the dock. Mr. Garland peered through the crack. "Whooeee," he said and whistled.

Ted flung himself down and looked too. And there, hanging on the end of Winkie's line, was the most enormous catfish he'd ever seen. It must have weighed twenty pounds and its wide ugly mouth and wicked barbels made it look as unpleasant as a shark. It was about two thirds out of the water and it shook its great body back and forth and tugged at the line.

"Oh, dear," panted Winkie.

"Let go of the line," Mr. Garland ordered. "Quick, Winkie, before he cuts your hands badly."

"Can I really let it go?" asked Winkie in a suddenly

interested voice. "It isn't my line and hook, you know, Uncle Ralph. It belongs to somebody else."

"Let go quick!" Mr. Garland repeated, and Winkie loosened her grip on the string and it slid from her hands. There was a loud splash as the catfish disappeared into the river.

"You had to let it go, Winkie," explained Bobbin kindly. "It was too big to pull up between the boards of the dock."

"Oh," said Winkie, wiping the blood from a cut on her left hand. "Well, I didn't know what to do. I didn't think I ought to just let it go off with the line and the hook. Besides, it was the first fish I ever caught."

It was Ted's line and hook. He'd left it there last week. He'd fished all Saturday with Steve and all he'd caught had been a couple of minnows which would have slipped between the boards of the dock with room to spare. He'd never even dreamed there were things like that catfish around.

"Winkie," said Mr. Garland, looking a little distracted, "how about staying away from the river unless some grownup is with you? Now let's go in and wash those cuts."

Winkie began to walk toward the house, but Ted stopped her. "What'd you use for bait?" he asked.

"Bubble gum," said Winkie.

And that was that. The twins went in, but Ted stayed outside. He went gloomily back to the tractor and worked over it till the sun began to set and the cold April twilight surged up out of the little hollows between the hills.

That night he lay awake a long time thinking over the day's events. Five whole days like today! He didn't think he could stand it.

"I ought to tell them the house is haunted," he thought. "I could rattle a few bones and chains around and maybe they'd think it was better to go stay with Grandmother. Or they might be so scared they'd just stay in bed all the time."

That wasn't a bad idea. He might just do that. He knew a good many stories about haunted houses and he could tell them without actually saying it was Five Owl Farm he was talking about. The twins would get the idea. He rolled over and contentedly went to sleep.

It was something of a surprise to him, then, when next morning at breakfast Bobbin suddenly announced, "Did you know this farm was haunted? Last night we saw the ghost."

ঙৌ Chapter Three

Ted raised startled eyes from his pancakes. But he
didn't look at Bobbin. Instead he gave his father a
long slow stare in which understanding and agreement
gradually took the place of surprise. Automatically
they both turned their heads toward the kitchen,
where Mrs. Garland was looking for more maple
syrup.

"Two minds with but a single thought," Mr. Garland said later. And the single thought was that
Mother might not exactly approve of what they were
about to do.

Mr. Garland cleared his throat. "Well, you're very
lucky," he said gravely. "Not many people get to *see*
the ghost. Of course we've all heard him at various
times. But not many people have seen him."

"What was it like?" asked Ted. "Where'd you see
him?"

Now it was the twins's turn to stare at each other.
They sat side by side like a pair of little corn-shuck

29

dolls with their noses almost touching, and finally Winkie said primly, "We don't believe in ghosts."

"No," said Bobbin instantly. "We don't believe in ghosts."

"Well, didn't you say you saw one?" queried Ted impatiently. "What'd you see, then? Why did you think it was a ghost? Where'd you see it?"

"We saw it out of Winkie's window," explained Bobbin. "I woke up and I remembered I put Freddy in Winkie's shoe while she was brushing her teeth. We're going to bury him today and he wouldn't be much good if she walked around on him, so I got up to tell her."

"And we heard a noise," Winkie went on.

"What kind of noise?" asked Mrs. Garland, coming in with the syrup.

"A—a—sort of—a—well, a ghost noise," said Bobbin. "Like a—like a wail. So we looked out the window and there was a blue light, it went just everywhere."

"It was in the barn," volunteered Winkie. "Only it came out and flew all around."

"Lightning?" asked Mrs. Garland. "I didn't see it."

"And then it went away," Winkie went on. "But we saw something come out of the barn and go creeping off. It was black and hunched up. It was kind of awful."

"It didn't have a head," Bobbin recalled. "Or legs or anything. It was just a kind of shape."

A little shiver ran down Ted's back. He couldn't help it. Maybe it was the way Winkie said "greeping" instead of "creeping." It was useless to tell himself there were no ghosts, and even if there were, no self-respecting ghost would show up where a couple of goofy twins could see it. Or so it seemed to Ted.

"Oh, nonsense," Mrs. Garland said. "It was all just your imagination. Just wind and shadows. Pass the twins the butter, Ted."

Ted passed the butter. "Well, I don't know," he began slowly. "Bob Fentress said his father said our barn was haunted. He spent the night there once, Bob's father, I mean, and he heard funny lights and saw queer noises. I mean—"

"Never mind," his mother interrupted firmly. "We all know what you mean and it's all twaddle. Any more black shapes coming out of the barn and we'll call the exterminator and put a stop to it. Now finish your breakfast and put your plates in the kitchen. And go make your beds if you haven't already done it. And fold the blankets neatly, Ted."

Ted gritted his teeth. He always folded his blankets neatly. He knew this was his mother's polite way of warning the twins that they must fold their blankets neatly, but it irked him terribly. She ought to just come right out and tell them. Not that it would do any good.

Now Cynthia leaned over and laid a skinny little hand on Mrs. Garland's arm. "We've made our beds, Aunt Priss," she said gently. "And we don't want to scare you, but we *did* see those things."

"Oh, dear," said Mrs. Garland. "Have some more

pancakes, Winkie. Maybe it's hunger that makes you see such things." And she smiled a smile that clearly said, "We'll humor the little dears but we won't take them seriously." It made Ted feel a little better.

Ted had already made his bed too and folded the blankets as neatly as he knew how. So when he'd helped clear the breakfast table, he followed his father onto the porch and watched while Mr. Garland gathered up papers and notes to take to work with him.

"Mother," he announced gloomily, "isn't going to be any help."

"She just doesn't want the twins frightened," said his father. "And neither do I. But I don't see any harm in a nice friendly ghost. Or better yet, a mystery. That's it, Ted, a nice friendly mystery. That ought to keep them busy and out of your hair without chilling their skinny little spines." He gave Ted a wink. "If they went to the barn and found a few clues lying around, that would no doubt give them food for thought. And still it wouldn't give them any more heebie-jeebies than they have ordinarily."

Ted considered. He hated parting with the ghost of Chief Five Owl. He'd spent a good deal of time concocting some pretty horrifying stories about him with which to entertain the twins. Of course he could still tell them if he wanted to. If his father was willing to supply the clues, Ted was willing to go along with a plain unadorned mystery.

He grinned. "I'll give up the ghost, Daddy," he said. "But you've got to come up with some neat clues.

Something really mysterious." He paused, thinking of
what kind of clues he'd leave if he were doing it, and
couldn't conjure up a thing. "I mean, not any ransom
notes or baby things like that!"

Mr. Garland gave him a sharp look. "Why not?"
he asked. "I thought you assumed the twins were
pretty backward mentally."

Ted opened his mouth to answer, not quite sure
what he was going to say, when the telephone rang
and Daddy dashed to answer it. He was always com-
plaining about people phoning, but Ted noticed he
was usually the first one to answer the phone's ring.
It came of being a newspaperman, Ted supposed.

When his father had gone to work, Ted called
Steve. "Don't come over for a few days," he warned.
"The twins are here."

"I can't come over," said Steve despairingly. "I'm in
bed."

"Why?" asked Ted.

"I got the mumps, I think," Steve answered. "At
least I've got a big swollen-up thing in my neck and
my mother thinks it's the mumps."

"It can't be the mumps!" cried Ted. "You had the
mumps once."

"Mother thinks it was Billy who had the mumps,"
Steve explained. Steve had four brothers and it was
hard sometimes to tell who had had what. "She ought
to write these things down," he added rather crossly.
"Once the doctor asked her how many teeth I had
and she said forty-eight and the doc nearly fainted."

"Oh. Yeah. Well," said Ted. How many teeth *did* people have, he wondered, running his tongue around among his molars. "Hurry and get over it, whatever it is. I'm almost sure you had the mumps in the first grade, so it must be something else. I want you to come over as soon as the twins leave."

"Well, I hope it's something else," said Steve. "Even the twins are better than the mumps."

Ted didn't know about that. He hung up and there they were, right behind him, like his own shadow.

"Why can't he come over before we leave?" asked Winkie.

"Twins give him a rash," answered Ted. "Why don't you two go out and play?"

"Aunt Priss said for you to take us around and show us where everything is," Bobbin explained.

"Well, this is the house, and that's outdoors, and there's the river," Ted pointed out. "Now you know where everything is, so leave me alone."

The twins stood side by side looking at him, and after a while he said in exasperation, "Oh, all right," and went and got his jacket and they all went out of the house.

The morning was cool and blue, with a sky as smooth and satiny as a robin's egg and only an occasional cloud floating across it. The gold-tasseled oaks and hickories, the new pale green of poplars, the pink and white and lavender of crab apple and haw and redbud, made the few pines and cedars look even darker and graver than ever.

Bluebirds burbled from the top of the house and swifts and one martin swooped and circled overhead. High up over the river two ducks went twinkling by. Ted drew a deep breath. Even the twins couldn't spoil all this.

"There's the barn," said Winkie, pointing.

"I know," Ted answered. "I live here."

"Let's go look at it," added Winkie after a minute.

"Why?" asked Ted.

"To see where the ghost was," explained Bobbin.

"I thought you didn't believe in ghosts," cried Ted. "Anyway it's just an old barn. And even if a ghost had been there, he wouldn't leave tracks or anything. Ghosts don't leave footprints. There wouldn't be anything to see. Just barn."

"I want to see the barn," said Winkie stubbornly.

"If it wasn't a ghost," pointed out Bobbin reasonably, "it was something else. And something else might leave tracks."

Ted didn't know how to answer this argument. He didn't want to take the twins into the barn this morning, not till his father had had a chance to plant some clues. But actually he didn't see how he was going to get out of it.

"We'd better ask Mother first," he said finally.

"We *asked* her," answered Winkie. "And she said it was all right, only not to go in the loft."

And that was that. Ted considered saying the twins could go ahead by themselves. Maybe they'd be scared to go alone. The only thing wrong with this theory was that the twins had already started off in the direction of the barn, and apparently they didn't care whether he came or not.

He had to run to catch up. However he reached the barn long before them. Bobbin and Winkie walked the way they did everything else, sort of on the bias, as Ted's father said. They zigzagged back and forth, inspecting a bunch of violets here, an interesting stone there, going back to look at a hole they were sure was a rabbit's hole, though Ted explained twice that it was where he'd pulled up a rotten fence post a few days before.

While he stood under the big oaks and waited for them in front of the barn, Ted went hastily through the pockets of his blue jeans, hoping to find something he could drop that would look like a clue. He was fairly certain Daddy hadn't come up here and planted any mysterious thumbprints or bloodstains around before he left for work.

His pockets held a clean handkerchief, two rubber bands, and some dusty orange Life Savers. Some clues! He was disgusted. Usually he had lots better things than that in his pockets. Just his luck, when he really needed something, not to have it.

He threaded one of the rubber bands through two of the candies and knotted it. It wasn't what *he'd* call a clue, but a couple of dopes like the twins might easily assume it was. He stuffed this arrangement back in his pocket and turned to find the twins standing in front of the barn door in some consternation.

Ted looked where they were looking and then he grinned a slow grin. He might have known he could count on Dad.

✿ Chapter Four

What the twins were staring at was a large bright new padlock. It was clasped firmly over the hasp on the great barn doors. Nobody was going in there. Ted almost chuckled aloud.

Winkie and Bobbin said nothing for several minutes. Then Bobbin spoke slowly and thoughtfully. "It must have been a ghost. We saw it open the door. If the door was locked, only a ghost could open it and walk outside."

"Maybe it had a key," put in Ted.

"To your barn?" asked Winkie.

"Sure," answered Ted. "Anybody can put a padlock on a door. I sure didn't put that one on. And it wasn't on last time I came up here. Anybody could have put it on, anytime."

"I expect somebody is using your barn for a hide-out," said Bobbin solemnly. "Maybe bank robbers."

"Or maybe car thieves," added Winkie. She pressed her face to a crack in the barn door. "I think I see a car in there."

Interested in spite of himself, Ted squinted through a crack too. But he couldn't see anything. It was very dim in the barn and it is a lot harder to look through a crack than people pretend it is. Anyway he could tell the place was all piled up with junk, discarded lumber and empty boxes and things. And he'd known that already.

"Let's go in," suggested Bobbin.

"How?" asked Ted scornfully. "Maybe ghosts can go through a locked door, but you can't."

"There's another door," Bobbin pointed out. "In the back. I saw it yesterday."

"But that doesn't go into the barn," said Ted. "It only goes into the shed." He didn't actually know this. He'd only glanced through that door to see that the shed was empty. He hadn't gone inside.

Anyway nothing he said was going to make any difference. The twins were already loping along under the hackberry trees to get to the other door.

Ted shrugged and followed. He had a feeling he was going to do lots of shrugging and following in the next few days. He was aware that somebody had to keep the twins from committing suicide by walking off the edge of a cliff, but he certainly wished it hadn't turned out to be his lot to do it.

The door to the lean-to at the back of the barn was not locked. It opened with a long rasping squeak that made Winkie shudder. Ted figured that ought to be a good ghostly sound to start exploring with.

He leaned forward and peered in over the twins'

heads. The sunlight slanted into the little room. It was quite empty and dust lay everywhere. There was no entrance into the barn, but there was a ladder nailed to the back wall. It disappeared into a small square hole in the ceiling.

"Look," said Bobbin in an impressive whisper, and Ted looked. The dust was thick on the rough floor, and here near the door there were several scuffed places that might easily have been a man's tracks.

"Footprints!" exclaimed Bobbin. "Or maybe it was just rats. There're always rats in barns."

Ted hated rats. They gave him a creepy-crawly sensation up his spine. He didn't know why. Maybe it was the way they sort of sneered and showed all their sharp teeth.

They all went on staring at the floor. There was a sudden loud snapping noise. Ted almost jumped. Winkie clutched his arm.

"What was that?" she whispered. "Is something there?"

"No, something isn't," answered Ted loudly. "Just a board creaking, probably. And there aren't any rats. Mother would have made Daddy get rid—"

Snap!

"There *is* something," Bobbin said softly. Together he and Winkie stepped up and entered into the lean-to. Ted watched. It wasn't rats. He was sure it wasn't rats. Maybe a mouse, but not a rat.

Snap!

"It's a slow clock," said Bobbin.

"It's a time bomb," announced Winkie. "I expect the car thieves want to blow up the barn to destroy the evidence."

"It isn't rats," Ted told himself. "Whoever heard of a ticking rat?"

He followed the twins inside and stood gazing around the dim little room. The snapping sound came again, from somewhere over the door. They all turned to look. There wasn't anything there except a few cobwebs. It was a little bit spooky.

"Ghosts," said Winkie briefly.

"There it is," cried Bobbin.

Once more Ted almost jumped, half expecting to see a headless figure "greeping" along.

But the twins had crowded up close to the wall and were gazing up into the spider webs.

"Where? Where?" asked Winkie.

"There, see?" Bobbin pointed into the midst of the maze of strings and cables. "A click beetle. I knew it was a click bettle."

Ted could see it now too, a medium-sized ordinary-looking brown beetle tangled in the web. And as they looked it contorted its body backward into an arch and then suddenly straightened out, making that loud click as its wing covers snapped into place.

Ted was amazed. "How'd you know what it was?" he demanded.

"He had one in the Frozen Fly Collection," answered Winkie.

"The what?" asked Ted.

"The Frozen Fly Collection," repeated Winkie. "Anyway that's what Daddy called it. But there were lots more things than flies in it."

"Well, what *was* it?" Ted almost shouted. How could anybody be so exasperating?

"It was Bobbin's," explained Winkie, as though that made everything clear. But seeing that Ted was still waiting, she went on. "He wanted to make an insect collection for school. We had a Science Fair."

"But the drug store wouldn't sell me any poison to kill them with," Bobbin went on. "And I didn't like to stick pins in their backs, like some people do. And then I remembered about freezing. Freezing doesn't hurt bugs, they just slow down till they just go so slow they die. So I took all my collection and put 'em in jars and stuck 'em in the freezer." He thought a minute. "I lost my best ants. They got behind the orange juice cans and I didn't find them till the fair was over."

"You mean it really worked?" Ted was astonished.

Bobbin considered. "It worked pretty well," he said at last. "It worked fine for beetles. But some of the other things got pretty mushy when they thawed. And one of the butterflies came alive after it was pinned in the box."

"It was terrible!" Winkie exclaimed. "I cried. But Mother stuck it back in the freezer and turned it down real low and Daddy said it probably didn't hurt it."

"That click beetle is bigger than my click beetle," Bobbin put in.

The children stared up at the web where the click beetle was now throwing itself about in great alarm and clicking like a typewriter. The spider had suddenly appeared from somewhere near the ceiling and was hanging head down among her ropes, surveying her victim meditatively.

The beetle struggled so desperately that Ted was moved to lend it a helping hand. Anyway he didn't think Winkie would like seeing the beetle murdered in cold blood. He raised his arm to try to reach the web, when the beetle with a final kick tore itself free from the threads and fell to the floor. It landed on its back and lay there waving its legs pathetically. And then once again it arched its body into a curve and with a final loud click snapped itself up into the air and landed right side up. Without a backward glance it trundled off into a crack in the floor boards.

"Oh, the poor spider," said Winkie mournfully. "Now it'll be hungry."

Ted stood there with his mouth open. There wasn't any use trying to figure out the twins. Who'd have imagined they'd be on the spider's side?

"We could bring it a fly," suggested Bobbin. "There was a sort of fly outside. I saw it."

Ted turned to leave. He might as well go work on the tractor. He certainly wasn't going to waste this lovely morning catching flies for any old spider. Right then Bobbin darted in front of him and snatched something from the floor.

"A clue!" he yelled. "A clue!"

As clues went, it wasn't so much. It was a small neat coil of very fine wire. Still Ted was a little puzzled about it. It looked new and clean, hardly even dusty. How did it come to be here? Had Daddy tossed it in here when he locked the barn doors? Ted didn't think he had. Daddy probably hadn't thought about the lean-to or supposed that the twins knew about it.

Not that it mattered much as long as the twins had something to mystify themselves with.

So while they turned it over and over, wondering and conjecturing, Ted planted his own clue. He dropped the Life Savers, tied in their rubber band, quietly to the floor.

He waited several minutes for the twins to notice, but they just went on inspecting the wire. Bobbin thought car thieves used wire for all sorts of things, like starting cars without keys, but he didn't know what kind of wire.

At last Ted couldn't stand it any longer.

"Let's see if there's anything else around," he suggested loudly. "Like car keys or more wire or—or something."

Winkie found the Life Savers at once.

"Look at this," she cried.

"Orange, my favorite," said Bobbin.

"Why are they tied up like that?" Winkie wondered.

"To keep them together," Bobbin assured her, and

she nodded. Then she untied the rubber band, dusted the candy on her T-shirt, handed one to Bobbin and popped the other in her mouth.

"Hey, don't eat those!" Ted yelled. "They might be poisoned or something. Anyway, what about me?"

"I didn't think you'd want one," Winkie answered around her Life Saver. "You threw them away, so I thought you must not like them."

Ted felt himself flush and hoped it was too shadowy in the shed for the others to notice.

Bobbin was now examining the ladder. "Let's go up," he suggested.

"Mother said not in the loft," Ted protested.

"That isn't the loft, is it?" inquired Bobbin. "Over this shed isn't the loft. The loft's over the barn. We can just look. We won't go in."

The hole in the ceiling looked very dark. Ted couldn't help thinking about rats.

"I'll go up and look first," he said.

"I ought to go first," said Winkie.

"Why?" asked Bobbin.

"Women and children first," Winkie stated. "And I'm women and children both. I'll go first."

And before Ted could stop her she had climbed the ladder like a little pale monkey and disappeared entirely.

Bobbin went after her. "Hey, wait!" called Ted. But there was nothing he could do except follow. It was getting to be a habit.

"It's dark," came Winkie's muffled voice. Bobbin

stopped and Ted surveyed the heels of his tennis shoes.

Ted took another step up. "Move on," he said impatiently to Bobbin. And then his hair almost stood on end.

From overhead there was a sudden rushing sound and then a moaning wail. Bobbin said "Oh!" loudly. Something growled, a fierce deep snarling growl, and Winkie screamed, "Help, oh, help!"

✐ Chapter Five

Ted was so scared he nearly fell off the ladder. The racket coming from the attic was like nothing he'd ever heard before, shrieks and snarls and squalls and thumps. Bobbin said "Oh!" once more and went rapidly up the last two steps of the ladder.

"Help, help, help, help!" bawled Winkie.

Ted mounted another rung of the ladder and tried to poke his head through the hole. But Bobbin had decided to retreat from whatever it was. He put his rubber-soled right foot firmly on Ted's head and stood there, waving the other leg about in space.

"Watch it, watch it!" bellowed Ted, trying to hold on to the ladder and clutch at Bobbin's legs at the same time.

"Help, help, help!" screamed Winkie.

"Oh, bother," said Bobbin. He put his left foot on Ted's shoulder, then slid down, and two seconds later he was clinging to his cousin's back and grasping Ted's hair with both hands.

48

"Oh, look out!" Ted yelled. "I'm going to fall! Jump, Bobbin, jump!"

But Bobbin stuck like a burr. Ted clawed at the ladder and then he and Bobbin were in a heap on the floor.

It wasn't much of a drop and Ted managed to catch a rung of the ladder and break the fall a little. He had twisted that arm and Bobbin's chin had come forward and hit him hard on the head, but the damage wouldn't have been so great if Winkie had not chosen that moment to make her escape from the attic. Still squealing "Help, help, help," she took the shortest way down. She simply jumped through the hole as if she was diving into a swiming pool. Ted and Bobbin were just struggling to their feet when she landed right on top of them.

It took a little while to sort themselves out. Bobbin's nose was bleeding freely. Winkie was rocking back and forth holding her ankles and moaning, and Ted was absolutely convinced his leg was broken. Well, anyway cracked. It was certainly going to have a really majestic bruise. And there was a long series of scratches down his arm and a knot on his head where Bobbin's bony chin had given it such a whack.

Ted hoped Bobbin had good strong teeth. Otherwise he was going to have to go to the dentist with crushed bicuspids.

"Give me your handkerchief, mine's used up," snuffled Bobbin.

Ted handed over his handkerchief and Winkie stopped rocking and looked on attentively.

"Do you think he'll bleed to death?" she asked as Bobbin continued to mop at his nose.

"I don't think so," Ted answered finally. "It looks like it's stopping. But I believe my leg's broken."

"Never mind," said Winkie kindly. "We'll read to you while you're in your cast. And bring you flowers and a basket of grapes, and Daddy said he'd get me a white mouse if Freddy was really dead, and I'll let you have it. Only you'll have to give it back when you get well."

"Oh, shut up," said Ted, heaving himself to his feet and moving his leg to see if it wasn't just a little bit cracked. It certainly felt like it. "What in the world got into you, jumping like that, Winkie? You might have killed us all. And, Bobbin, you aren't much better. Next time you want to climb down a ladder, let me know and I'll get out of the way."

Bobbin sniffed.

"Winkie wanted to come down," he pointed out. "I had to get out of the way."

"Well, you got out of the way and I got out of the way," Ted said. "So how come she didn't come down the ladder? How come, huh? What'd she have to jump for?"

"I was in a hurry," said Winkie. "Jumping seemed like the quickest thing to do."

Bobbin leaned forward. "What was up there?" he

asked in a voice stifled by the bloody handkerchief. "What made all that racket?"

Winkie's eyes grew bigger. "It was dreadful," she whispered. "It was awful. I was scared. It was big and made such scary awful noises. It was all over every-where. It was awful."

"What was it?" asked Bobbin, whispering too. "Was it a ghost? What was it, Winkie?"

Winkie put her hands up to her thin little face. "It was dreadful," she repeated. "I was so scared. It was—gruesome."

She took her hands down and said in a normal voice, "It was an owl. Or maybe two owls. I couldn't see."

"Owls!" cried Ted. "Neat-o! I thought maybe this barn had owls in it." Actually he hadn't thought any such thing, but now that it had occurred to him, what better place for barn owls than a barn?

He zipped up the ladder. It was dark in the sloping space under the roof, as Winkie had mentioned. She had not, however, said anything about how hot and smelly it was. "Phew!" said Ted. He tried to stand up but he couldn't manage because of the slanting roof and the beams. He had to sort of crouch while his eyes grew used to the dimness.

The owls were gone. There was only a handful of soft gray and brown feathers on the floor. A sort of window leading into the barn loft had been cut into the wall between the shed and the barn and Ted fig-

urd the owls had gone out that way. He peered into the loft, but he didn't go in for a number of reasons. Of course the owls would mean there weren't any rats in the barn. Probably. But he'd wait till he had a flashlight. Mother said the loft was dangerous, the boards could be rotted through anywhere.

"Ted?" called Winkie anxiously. "Are you coming down?"

"Just a minute," Ted answered. Maybe he could find something up here, something mysterious he could show the twins for a clue. But the feathers and some dry leaves and dust and cobwebs were all he could see.

Oh, well, it had all been mystifying and scary. Ted had been mystified himself, a little. Not scared, like the twins. Just puzzled.

He wished he'd been the one to see the owls.

He came down the ladder and collected the twins. The three of them went out of the shed and slowly circled the barn, pressing their faces to the cracks and trying to see into the lightless interior.

The barn was in better shape than Ted had thought. He couldn't find any rotten boards or broken places. Mother must be wrong when she called it a "tumbledown" place and said it was dangerous.

Winkie saw all kinds of things through the cracks, figures and flapping wings, a pile of machine guns and a bag labeled "First National Bank."

"She's only saying those things," Bobbin told Ted. "It's a kind of game. She doesn't really see them."

"You're kidding," said Ted sarcastically, and then

he was sorry. The trouble was he couldn't make up his mind whether to be exasperated with the twins for being silly enough to believe in all this foolishness or for having too much sense to be taken in by it. "We'd better go home. It'll be lunchtime soon."

"Oh, boy," said Bobbin. "I'm hungry."

Ted looked at the two little figures in front of him, streaked with dust and blood, and suddenly realized he couldn't take them home like that. Mother would put her foot down on the barn—and hard. He'd never have a chance to show them Daddy's clues.

"Wait a minute," he said and considered. Not the river, that wouldn't do. But, oh, yes, down there on the hillside beyond the wall that edged the old orchard there was a spring. Mr. Garland had warned Ted not to drink out of it till the water had been tested, but they had both rinsed the mud from their hands in it the other day. It was plenty good to wash in.

On the way they passed a little thicket of azalea just beginning to bloom well. Ted had some trouble getting the twins away from it. They were fascinated by the exotically shaped flowers in all their many shades of pink.

"It smells so delicious it makes me want to bite something," sighed Winkie.

Now that was the kind of dumb thing the twins would say. But maybe in a way she was right. Ted ran his tongue surreptitiously over his lips. The fragrance was so thick and sweet in the air it did seem as though you ought to be able to taste it.

At the spring Ted washed everybody's handkerchiefs and then their faces. The water was clear and icy and full of bubbles. Winkie kept leaning over and plunging her hands into the little rocky basin. Twice she nearly fell in.

"Would you stop acting like an idiot for just two seconds and wash your face?" Ted asked impatiently, holding his handkerchief soaked in cold water against the lump on his head.

"I'm washing," answered Winkie, leaning forward to look at her reflection and almost losing her balance. Ted sighed.

He made them comb their hair with wet fingers and he got Bobbin to button his sweater across his chest and hide most of the bloodstains on his T-shirt. Now maybe they looked respectable enough to go home. Maybe he could sneak them up the stairs before his mother got a close look at them. The trouble with being so fair, as the twins were, was that every spot showed so plainly. Ted was glad of his own dark brown hair and freckled face.

Mrs. Garland didn't seem to notice anything special when they came in. Ted shoved the twins upstairs and persuaded them to change their shirts and use some soap before lunch. He stuffed Bobbin's bloody T-shirt in the back of his closet. Maybe he would get a chance to wash it himself before they left for home.

After lunch Ted would have been quite willing to lie down on his bed and read his library book. It was a pretty good one, about pioneers and Indians, and he was at a very exciting part.

Anyway his leg ached and both his arms were sore and he would have liked a rest.

But his mother asked him to come out in the yard and help her move some rocks and there wasn't much he could do but go. The sun shone bright and hot, the breeze had died down, and moving the rocks turned out to be quite a workout. Ted kept consoling himself with the thought of how fast his muscles were developing.

The twins helped. Ted was surprised. The twins never seemed to get tired. And they could move almost any rock, no matter how big.

But as usual they were far from efficient. Once Bobbin dropped a rock, a big one, and it missed Ted's foot by about one thirty-seventh of an inch. And when Bobbin thought he'd found a snake, instead of putting her rock down and going to look, Winkie staggered across the yard still clutching a huge boulder in her hands.

And then of course she had to carry it all the way back to where it was supposed to go. And the snake turned out to be just an extra big earthworm.

The sun shone and Ted sweated.

"Goodness," exclaimed Mrs. Garland, "you can almost see things growing. And doesn't the narcissus smell wonderful?"

Winkie's nose was already bright yellow with pollen from smelling various flowers.

"But if this heat keeps up, nothing will last any time," Mrs. Garland went on, frowning. "My hyacinths are all drooping and the forsythia's just about gone."

Ted deposited the last of the rocks in the spot where his mother wanted them and flopped on the grass. The sun felt marvelous and he just lay there, while the twins buzzed around him like a couple of skinny white bees. They asked the names of all the flowers and Bobbin pointed out two helpful kinds of insects. He really knew a good deal about bugs.

"Ted," said his mother suddenly, "how about taking a bath and getting cleaned up before Daddy gets home?"

Ted thought about saying he was clean enough and then he changed his mind. A bath wasn't a bad idea, and he was almost sure he could get away from the twins in the tub and not have them pestering him for a while.

He got up from the grass and started in the house, and the twins came right after him. Would you believe it? They were going to stick with him right on through his bath and everything!

He was turning around to tell them to beat it, when the telephone rang. Ted picked up the receiver and it was his father. He said, "Ted? Tell Mother I won't be home for supper. I won't be home till late, maybe ten o'clock or even later. I'll call her if I can."

"Okay, Dad," Ted answered. He was going to say something about the padlock on the barn door, but the twins were standing right at his elbow. So he hung up without saying anything more.

He was sorry his father wasn't coming home. There'd been a time in his life when having Daddy stay late at the paper had sort of scared him. It made him think there was going to be a war or an explosion or something. By this time he'd learned it was much more likely to be something like a piece of machinery breaking down.

Once, Ted remembered, lightning had struck the newspaper building and burned up a lot of stuff and made a mess of his father's desk. And once three of the printers had come down with mumps all at the same time and his father hadn't been able to come home for two whole days.

It was probably something like that now. But Ted had looked forward to having his father help entertain the twins this evening and get them in the proper mystery mood by telling a few of the wild tales he was good at making up.

And Ted had planned once again to do some reading after supper; those Indians were still in hot pursuit of the pioneers. But somehow after a late meal and helping clear the table, he felt too tired and sleepy and sore to read. Instead he had a fierce argument with Bobbin about whether pronghorn antelopes shed their horns or not. And since he was secretly afraid that Bobbin knew more about antelopes than he did, he got up suddenly and went to bed. He was asleep in two minutes.

He was having a confused dream about keeping
antelopes in the barn when something woke him.
Startled, he sat up in bed and the two small white figures standing beside him nearly scared him into a
fit. He'd forgotten about the twins.

"Good grief," he cried. "Can't you even let me sleep
in peace? What do you want?"

"Come in Winkie's room, quick," whispered
Bobbin.

Ted scrambled out of bed. Whatever was going on,
he wanted to know.

It was moonlight. From Winkie's window he could
see the front of the barn through the trees.

"What is it?" he asked. "What's happened?"

"Nothing," Bobbin answered.

Ted could hardly believe his ears. "Then how come
you woke me up?" he cried.

"Wait," whispered Winkie. "Something's going to
happen."

Ted groaned. "Something's going to happen, all
right," he said. "I'm going back to bed. And I'm probably going to catch cold from standing around in my
pajamas."

"Something really will happen, I expect," said
Bobbin calmly. "Lots of times when Winkie says something is going to happen, something does."

"Well, tell me about it tomorrow," growled Ted,
when Winkie whispered sharply, "There! There!"

Ted pulled back the curtains. He couldn't see a
thing, just the barn and the trees.

And then suddenly he saw it. There was a light in the barn door and then something stood there, a big horrible headless shapeless sort of mass standing in the barn door!

◦ℰ Chapter Six

Ted stared. What in the world could it be? What was making that queer light shining softly all around it? The thing moved. All at once the glow vanished. They could just make out the hulking body as it moved away under the trees and then disappeared entirely.

"Well," said Winkie smugly. "Something happened."

"Yes," agreed Bobbin. "I thought it would."

"But what was it?" asked Ted. "What did happen?"

It was a weird thing. He'd ask Daddy how he did it. But if they planned on taking the twins' minds off ghosts, his father was making a mistake. That was as ghostly an item as Ted ever saw. It certainly didn't look like bank robbers or car thieves.

The twins didn't answer. They crouched by the window, waiting for what would happen next. They waited for ten minutes, and then the only thing that happened was that Winkie sneezed and Ted yawned.

"We'd better go back to bed," he said.

"What we ought to do is go out there," said Bobbin. "At night, I mean. Everything's locked up in the daytime and nothing's going on. If we want to find out about it, we ought to go out after dark."

"Now," said Winkie. "Let's go now."

"You're out of your skull," said Ted. "If you're going to do a thing like that, you've got to lay plans and take equipment and decide on strategy and things. What we ought to do now is go to bed and get a good night's sleep." It would never do to have the twins traipsing around in the dark and maybe running into Daddy.

"I've got my big flashlight," said Bobbin. "That's equipment. And we can plan to go up to the barn and look around and come back. That's plans. I don't see why we'd need anything else."

"I expect we'd need a weapon," said Winkie.

"No," said Bobbin solemnly, "some innocent person might get hurt. If anybody comes after us, I'll hit 'em with my big flashlight."

They really were planning to go! Ted was astonished. Were they really as brave as all that? Or were they just too dumb to know when to be scared?

Anyway he couldn't let them go out. Not now. They might meet Daddy or find out how he was doing these things, whatever they were. He'd have to stop them. "Even if you had a weapon, you couldn't shoot a ghost or stop it or anything," he pointed out. "You couldn't even hit one with a flashlight."

"I think it's a monster," said Winkie. "Somebody is hiding a monster in the barn and lets it out on moonlit nights."

"I don't think it's a monster," Bobbin answered. "And I don't think it's a ghost, either. I think it's car thieves. And they want us to think it's a ghost or a monster so we won't go near the barn. At least that's the way it is in books," he added a little less certainly.

He and Winkie turned toward the door.

"Where are you going?" asked Ted loudly.

"Hush," whispered Winkie. "You'll wake Aunt Priss. We're going back to look in the barn. We'll be all right. We'll take Bobbin's big flashlight."

"Listen," cried Ted, "are you crazy or something? You can't go running around in the dark like that."

"We won't run," said Bobbin. "We'll walk very carefully. If you're afraid, you don't have to come. We'll be all right."

Ted was helpless with rage. "Of course I'm not scared," he retorted, speaking between gritted teeth. "But Mother wouldn't like you two batting around in the dark."

"Oh, she won't mind," said Bobbin. "We won't go in the loft."

"And we'll have Bobbin's big flashlight," repeated Winkie.

Resigned, Ted went back to his room to get his bathrobe and followed them out of the room. It didn't really matter, he reflected as he and Winkie waited for Bobbin to find his big flashlight. As long as he was along to keep them from falling in the river, they were safe enough. There wasn't anything here on the farm to hurt anybody. And he was sure by this time his father had gotten the barn locked up tight again.

They slipped softly down the stairs and past his parents' bedroom door and out on the front porch. The front door wasn't locked which was proof enough, Ted thought, that there was nothing to fear here on the farm. Rosemary's cat, Squintina, was asleep on the banisters.

Bobbin's big flashlight was indeed big. It was two feet long, at least, and heavy and efficient-looking. The only trouble was that it gave about as much light as a lightning bug.

"It needs new batteries," Bobbin explained. "I'm going to start saving money for them pretty soon."

"Well, you'd better hurry," said Ted grimly. "I don't think these are going to last till we get to the barn."

Not that they needed its light. The moon, almost full, made it seem bright as day. Every now and then a cloud, thin and rippled like an old quilt whose stuffing has settled between the stitching, slid over the moon, and then the shadows melted and sagged and spread out from under the trees. But the clouds were small and infrequent and most of the time Ted could see almost as well as though it were the middle of the day.

The path to the barn twisted along the slope, easy to follow in the moonlight. The buds on the trees stood out, fat and silver. And once they walked under a dogwood tree and the moonlight spilled down through its blossoms, making them wider and whiter than in daylight. Winkie and Bobbin turned their pale faces up to the pale light and, in their white bathrobes and white pajamas, they looked like a couple of little statues.

It was cool but far from cold. The little wind that moved the clouds had a softness and freshness like rain water. It brought the children the odd sharp smell of the river banks and the sweet smell of new growing things and a whiff or two of warm pine needles. The chorus of frogs was silent, but now and then one called sleepily, a sweet purring note.

Somewhere close to the river a mockingbird began to sing. Ted was suddenly very glad the twins had decided to investigate the barn.

"Is that an owl?" asked Winkie.

"No, pea brain." Ted was scornful. "Owls don't sing. It's a mockingbird."

"I didn't mean singing," said Winkie with dignity. "I meant there."

She pointed up to the top of one of the pear trees. There was certainly something there, a sort of dark blob. Ted wasn't sure it was anything to bother about. It could just as easily be somebody's old dead kite as an owl. The children stood watching until the blob suddenly shook itself and came sailing down right at them.

The twins dodged as though they might actually have been white rabbits. The owl swooped over Ted's head, so close he could feel the rush of its passage rippling his hair, and then it was gone, disappearing into the mingled moonlight and shadow of the night.

Ted felt a little shiver up his backbone. Close as

that owl had come to him, it had been absolutely silent. The air had stirred, he had felt it, but it had stirred soundlessly. As though a ghost had passed. No wonder people were scared of owls. Ted wondered how in the world owls managed to do it.

"An owl," said Bobbin with awe. "A real owl."

"Well, it sure wasn't stuffed," Ted answered and looked up at the sky. A big heavy black cloud had appeared from nowhere and was sliding steadily toward the moon. If they didn't hurry they were going to have to rely on Bobbin's flashlight to see by and that wasn't much to rely on.

"Let's go look for the owl," suggested Winkie. "Maybe we could catch it. We could take it home with us and keep it in the attic. And feed it mice and things. And make a nest—and—"

Bobbin started off immediately, waving his flashlight around like an anemic will-o'-the-wisp. Ted ran after him and seized him by the shoulder.

"Where do you think you're going?" he asked crossly. "I thought you wanted to go look in the barn. If you don't come on, I'm going back to bed."

"Oh, all right," said Bobbin and shrugged. "Anyway, I like mice. I wouldn't want to feed them to an owl. I'd rather tame a mouse than an owl, I think."

"Mice," repeated Winkie. "There're lots of mice around here. Let's go catch a mouse."

"Hold on," roared Ted. "Don't you two have any sense? If you aren't going to the barn, let's go back to bed."

"That's right, Winkie," Bobbin said. "We can catch mice any time."

"If we caught a mouse," Winkie went on dreamily, "Daddy wouldn't have to buy me a white mouse. That would save a lot of money, I think. Freddy cost ninety-eight cents and that's a lot of money."

Ted was just getting ready to shout again, when something happened. Bobbin's big flashlight flickered and died.

"Oh, dear," said Winkie.

"Oh, darn!" said Bobbin.

"Rats!" said Ted.

The big black cloud was rapidly approaching the moon. Its filmy edge was already creeping into the circle of the moon's light, forming an iridescent and rainbow-colored ruffle about the ominous darkness. Above the children on the hill the barn loomed shadowy and threatening. The wind was rising. A branch of one of the oak trees scraped along the barn roof, making an eerie rasping noise.

"Let's go home," said Winkie.

"No," said Bobbin firmly. "We ought to finish what we started out to do. Daddy always says that, you know he does."

"Well, come along then," cried Ted. "If you don't hurry, it's going to get so dark we won't be able to see anything, if there's anything to see—which I doubt."

"Just a minute," said Bobbin. He shook his flashlight a couple of times and then unscrewed the end of it and squinted down at the batteries. He spit on his finger and rubbed it on the end of the cell and then replaced the metal cap and shook it again. Nothing happened.

"They're really dead, I guess," he said mournfully. He took Winkie's hand. "Come along."

"Well, at last!" exclaimed Ted.

They climbed the hill toward the barn. The night grew darker and darker. The wind blew in sudden rushing gusts and the branches of the huge oak by the barn door waved about wildly and sent a shower of pollen down on them. It made Ted sneeze.

"Look there," whispered Winkie. Something big and white went scuttling by, close to the fence.

"It's only a sheet of newspaper," Ted answered.

"Well, how did it get out here?" whispered Winkie. "It didn't come out here all by itself."

They stood watching it slowly move down the hillside, making sort of snaky motions, up and down, up and down, until it finally blew against a bush and settled to the ground.

"I guess it's dead now," said Winkie more cheerfully. "We can go on."

"The door's open this time," Bobbin said. Ted looked. He couldn't tell whether it was open or not. The whole front of the barn was in deepest shadow. But Bobbin had sounded confident enough.

Why would his father leave the door open? Had he planted some clues for them to find in the morning? Should Ted make the twins turn back now?

He couldn't think of any way to do it. Instead, with

Bobbin on one side and Winkie on the other, he crept step by step, closer and closer to the barn door. It *was* open, he was almost certain. Overhead the wind sang a queer little high-pitched song in the oak branches. Ted wished he'd asked his mother about rats, about whether there really were any in the barn.

His heart thumped. It was a little scary. Well, it was a *lot* scary, out here in the pitch dark and the wild night, with that big black shape of the barn humping up in front of them.

Suddenly Winkie gave a wild scream. "Horrible, horrible!" she shrieked.

"The ghost!" yelled Bobbin and dashed ahead.

There was a blue-white blinding flash and Ted flung his arm across his eyes!

❧ Chapter Seven

A galaxy of whirling planets and flashing stars spun and floated before Ted's sight. Something moaned, something small and furry brushed by his pajama leg—was it a rat?—and Ted staggered backward, pressing his hands to his face.

"Bobbin!" he cried. "Winkie!" but there was no answer. Only the high sad sound of the wind, and way off somewhere a scuffling confused noise. Ted took his hands from his dazzled eyes and strained to see. Gradually the blaze of lights died away but still he could make out only the dimmest shapes of trees and barn. He put out his hands and felt around in the dark, and something strange brushed against his fingertips. He jumped and almost yelled and stood there, half waiting to be grabbed by a—well, by he didn't know what.

But he kept thinking about Bob Fentress's father and the things he claimed to have seen in the barn.

"Bobbin," he called.

Nothing answered. The wind swooped down suddenly, rocking the limbs of the trees, and one or two of the oak tassels drifted down on him. Their feathery touch made him start again.

He shook himself. There wasn't any ghost, or any monster either. Whatever that light was, it was just some trick his father had rigged up. Probably. And now the thing for him to do was stop leaping like a grasshopper every time the wind blew, find the twins, and get back home and into bed.

Slowly he moved forward to the yawning emptiness, blacker than the rest of the blackness, that marked the barn door. He leaned on the edge of the door frame and peered into the barn. He couldn't see a thing.

"Bobbin!" he said softly. "Winkie!"

Something stirred in the barn, a rustling ruffling sound. Was it an owl? Was it rats? Ted's toes curled inside his slippers. He did hate rats.

Well, it wasn't ghosts anyway. He was certain of that. He took a slow careful step inside the barn. "Cynthia!" he called, more loudly.

Once again there was that sound of something moving in the murky corners of the barn. *Whish, whish, whish, shwee shirka* . . . that was what it sounded like. Like something soft brushing against something rough, agitated and alert. It made Ted uneasy.

There was no other answer. If the twins were in there, somebody or something was keeping them silent.

Now that was nonsense. The twins weren't the brightest people in the world, but even they weren't so dumb as to go running straight into an unlighted building which they were convinced was filled with ghosts or monsters. They must have run the other way.

Ted drew a deep breath. He'd hunt for them awhile outside, but if he couldn't find them pretty soon, he'd have to go get his father. He turned and stepped out of the barn. Behind him there was for a third time a little scratchy chorus of sighs and slitherings and he whirled around and walked backward away from the door. He knew it was silly, but he couldn't help it. He didn't like all that black nothingness staring out at the back of his neck. He wished the moon would come out again.

He couldn't go very fast backward. He couldn't exactly gallop when he faced the way he was going, because of the dark and the uncertain footing on the path down the rough hillside. But there was something about his legs that didn't work properly going in reverse. He was making about a half mile an hour and he'd be the rest of the night getting home. He didn't see why you couldn't walk backward as well as forward. It looked as if you ought to be able to go as fast one way as the other. Then it dawned on him that his knees only bent in one direction.

He was so busy thinking this through that he forgot about the barn and just went on walking backward until he stumbled over something and nearly fell. He spread out his arms to regain his balance and touched something damp and cold and soft and hard at the same time.

He yelped and snatched his hand away and then realized it must be one of the moss-covered rocks in the old tumble-down wall that ran along below the pear trees. Gosh, he was way off the track. He was going to get lost if he wasn't careful.

He glared hard into the darkness trying to judge which way to go. It was curious what a difference the moonlight had made. The hillside which had looked so beautiful and dreamlike when the moon was out now just looked grim, with shadowy shapes that might or might not be moving. And the dogwoods were sort of pale scary spots in the night.

Ted concluded he wasn't as familiar with this part of the farm as he had thought he was. Or else the dark changed things around. He wished he'd had sense enough to leave a light on in his bedroom so that now he'd be able to spot the house. As it was he was in the pitch-black dark. There wasn't a street light for miles and miles. There were two other houses close enough to see, but the farmers who lived in them went early to bed. No gleam showed from either of them to help him get his bearings.

There was a movement off to one side and he froze, peering into the gloom. Was it just a bush, swaying in the wind that came and went over the hillside? There was a sound like slow heavy footsteps and Ted's heart thumped. There *was* something over there, he was sure! Something headless and shapeless, creeping along. He crouched, waiting. But nothing happened, and after a while he banged himself on the head with his fist and told himself to quit being a dope. If there was anything out here, it was a stray cow and nothing more. The only danger he was in was the danger of falling over a rock or tree root.

He set out once again to find the path. He went along cautiously, but twice he ran into trees before he knew they were there. Once he looked up to see somebody standing over him with upraised arms.

For a minute he was too scared to move and then he realized it was just that broken apple tree. It helped him get his bearings, and as soon as he got on the path he flew toward the house. He had to get his father. He knew the twins must be somewhere out there, lost and frightened, probably paralyzed with fright. He'd been pretty scared himself and he was older than the twins and had a lot more sense. He should have known better than to let them come on an expedition like this.

The moon came out as he neared the house. "Wouldn't you know?" he asked himself. "Now it's too late to be a help."

Squintina was no longer on the porch, but something was lying on the steps. Something long and pale and sinister, like an albino snake. Ted bent over it.

It was the belt from one of the twins' bathrobes. They had come straight home then! He wondered how they'd managed in the dark.

And then he was angry. They'd just run off and left him to face whatever it was, alone and without Bobbin's big flashlight, even let him flounder around looking for them, half killing himself on various trees and rocks! He ought to break their skinny little necks.

He slipped through the front door and up the stairs. In their respective beds Bobbin and Winkie were sleeping soundly. Ted flung himself into his own bed, planning to stay awake for hours and hours and figure out some revenge, but he was far too tired. The next thing he knew it was broad daylight.

He was tired and aching and as cross as three sticks. His arm was sore and his head hurt to touch. He stuck his leg out from under the covers and there was indeed a ghastly blue and green bruise down his shin. Even though it was going to be another warm day, he'd have to wear blue jeans, because if he wore shorts his mother would be sure to investigate that bruise.

He looked up at the window and realized suddenly that it must be late in the morning. He struggled out of bed and got washed and dressed and went downstairs.

It was strangely quiet. Squintina was in the kitchen asleep in a chair, but Ted couldn't find anybody else. Several people had eaten breakfast, for the table plainly showed the evidence—some rumpled mats, a lot of crumbs, a platter with about a half teaspoon of scrambled eggs on it, and a cup of cold coffee.

He stood frowning down at a blob of marmalade on one of the mats, feeling neglected and peeved and frustrated all at once. He'd kind of looked forward to being snappish with the twins at breakfast, and now everybody had forgotten him and eaten all the bacon and eggs and there was nobody to snap at but Squin-tina, who merely yawned, showing a great many sharp teeth, and went back to sleep.

Ted went out to the glassed-in porch which served his father as a study and stared through the many windows at the river. The day was hazy, it was going to be hot again. The big sugar maples near the river were covered with new vivid green leaves that only a few days ago had been tight buds.

Did spring always go by this fast? Ted wondered. He hadn't ever noticed it before. The front door opened and someone came in. It was his mother. He heard her walking in the hall.

"Oh, are you up?" she exclaimed when he stalked into the dining room. "I thought you'd still be in bed. You were sleeping so soundly. Did the twins wake you?"

"The twins aren't here," he answered glumly.

Mother frowned. "Not here?" she repeated. "Then where are they? Oh, dear, I might have known. It was so hot and sunny, I just had to go out and put paper caps over those seedlings I set out yesterday. And the twins were eating breakfast—I had no idea they'd finish so soon. Ted, go find them. I don't like not knowing where they've wandered off to. They shouldn't have gone out without telling me."

"But I haven't had my breakfast," Ted protested. He was pretty sure he knew where the twins were.

"Well, I'll have to cook some eggs and bacon for you," Mrs. Garland pointed out. "That'll take a few minutes. All I want is to know where they are and to tell them not to go too far from the house. Run, find them, and I'll squeeze you an extra big glass of orange juice."

She went on into the kitchen and Ted heard her mutter, "Eight pieces of toast? Heavens, how do they manage to eat so much?"

He clattered out the front door and down the steps. The sun was really hot and the bees in the lilacs made a summery sound. When he walked under the dogwoods the blossoms had begun to shatter and there was a circle of petals on the ground. Only his mother said they weren't really petals, they were something else. He picked one up. They certainly looked like petals.

The twins, as he had predicted, were at the barn. The door was once more shut and fastened. But the twins had been busy. They had accumulated a little heap of things and piled them on the ground in front of the barn door. "Clues," explained Bobbin solemnly. There was some string, a small bag of sunflower seeds, a piece of paper with lines and circles drawn on it, a sponge, and an apple with one bite out of it.

Winkie pointed to the sponge. "I guess that's what I stepped on," she said. "Last night, I mean."

Ted remembered. That must have been when she had moaned out, "Horrible, horrible!" A sponge would be kind of a nasty thing to step on in the dark. He stepped on it to see, and it was squishy and kind of horrible.

He poked at the apple with his foot. Now what kind of clue was that? To be honest, he thought Daddy could have come up with something a lot better than this if he'd really tried. Of course, he'd been down at the newspaper so much, perhaps he hadn't been able to do any better.

"Come on home," Ted said a little crossly. "Mother doesn't want you wandering around by yourself. And I haven't had any breakfast. And I'm starved."

"You could have the rest of the apple," suggested Winkie and he glared at her.

"Come on," he yelled.

Meekly Bobbin and Winkie gathered up the clues and followed Ted down the hill.

Ted was finally getting his breakfast—and really wolfing it down—when the phone rang. "Get that, would you please, Ted?" called Mrs. Garland. Ted dashed toward the hall, swallowing his piece of toast sidewise and only just managing to squeak "Hello" into the mouthpiece.

"Ted, is that you?" It was his father's voice. "You sound so queer."

Ted glanced hurriedly over his shoulder. For once the twins hadn't followed. "Daddy," he said hoarsely, "about the clues. The lights are fine but—"

"Put those on my desk, will you, Pete?" his father said, evidently addressing somebody with him. "Ted, have you got a sore throat? I can't understand you."

"About the clues—" began Ted once more.

"On second thought, Pete, you'd better take them

on downstairs," Mr. Garland went on. "What, Ted? Oh, the clues!" He paused and then said slowly, "I'm sorry, Ted. What with all the excitement here at the paper, I just forgot all about clues. We'll see what we can do later. Now let me speak to your mother."

"Yessir," said Ted. And he put the phone down on the table and stared at it very thoughtfully indeed.

✐ Chapter Eight

When Ted got back to the breakfast table, the twins were sitting there eating his toast. "Lay off," he yelled. "You've had your toast."

"We thought you'd left," explained Winkie. "You went away."

"The telephone rang. I went to answer it. At my mother's request," explained Ted in the deliberate tones of a boy who is doing his very best to keep from swatting a small female cousin. "Anybody with a half ounce of brains would know I was coming back."

"How would they know?" asked Winkie in an interested voice, and Ted was about to give in to his impulse to squash her when Bobbin looked up with a frown from the paper he was studying.

"Does 'mi' stand for miles?" he asked.

The paper was the one the twins had found at the barn. Ted looked at it with considerably more interest than he had before his phone conversation with his father.

It wasn't really a paper, it was one of those stiff note

cards, plain on one side and narrowly lined on the other. A sort of diagram was drawn in heavy inked strokes on the plain side.

There were four small circles, and leading from each circle straight lines labeled things like "7¼ h 30 ver". At the bottom of the card there were some words, or sort of words: 3 mi 1 gshpr? 1 nstlg.

"It's in German, I expect," said Bobbin. "Or Korean or Czechoslovakian or something."

"Spies!" cried Winkie. "Spies!"

"There's nothing around here to spy on," said Ted.

"Yes, there is," answered Bobbin quickly. "There's the river and all those boats going up and down. Uncle Ralph said some of them were carrying parts and material for defense plants. And there's the dam and the powerhouse and all."

"I guess you're right," Ted admitted. He and Bobbin gazed silently at the chart for a long time.

That could be what the chart was about, Ted told himself. For all he knew, nstlg was Russian for dam. "Is there anything on the back?" he asked.

Bobbin turned the card over. Scrawled across the card was the one word APPLES in big letters.

"That's not German," said Winkie. "That's English."

"Wow!" said Ted. "What a genius!"

But his heart wasn't in the sarcasm. The truth of the matter was he was feeling a little worried and even scared. Last night had he and the twins been up against something real, somebody who might truly have been a threat to them? And he was the one who'd been in greatest danger, who'd been up there so long all by himself and even stepped inside the barn and heard those sinister noises. He whistled softly.

"What's the matter?" asked Bobbin, and just then Mrs. Garland came into the dining room.

"Ted," she said, "Daddy says he'll be home around noon. And he wants to walk up to the top of that north hill and locate the property line, and he wants us to come with him. It's so warm I'm afraid it's going to rain, but I'm wild to get up in those woods and see what's blooming, so we'll risk it. And if it doesn't rain, when we get back we'll cook supper outdoors on the grill. How'll that be? Frankfurters and marshmallows."

The twins said nothing. They sat side by side, looking very blank. But even Ted could tell they were disapproving of something.

"Don't you want to go hiking?" asked Mother.

"Don't you like hot dogs?" asked Ted at the same moment.

For a minute the twins just sat on. But finally Winkie said, "Bobbin doesn't eat hot dogs."

"Oh," said Mrs. Garland.

"Gosh, anybody who doesn't like hot dogs must be out of their skulls," said Ted.

"He likes hot dogs, he just doesn't eat them," said Winkie.

There was a short silence. Ted and his Mother looked at Bobbin and Winkie, and the twins looked gravely back.

"They have buttons in them," explained Bobbin at last.

"What?" cried Mother.

"Once, at school, he found a button in his hot dog. So he doesn't eat them anymore," Winkie went on.

"It was a blue button," added Bobbin darkly.

"Well, good grief, I never found a button in my hot dogs and I've eaten thousands and thousands," Ted spoke up.

"Never mind," said Mother hastily. "We'll have hamburgers. It's all the same to me. Daddy'll be here about noon, Ted. Do you want lunch? You've had such a late breakfast, I didn't think you'd want lunch."

He didn't but the twins did, naturally. He thought while they were eating he'd slip out and take a really good look at the barn. Maybe he'd find a way to get inside. He might go through the shed and into the loft. After all, if something funny was going on—and it must be—you had to take a few risks, like stepping on a rotten place in the loft floor and falling through.

It was his own fault that he didn't get to do it. He took his time climbing the rough path to the barn, looking around at all the changes a warm night had worked on the landscape. The hills behind the barn were turning from gold to green as the oak and hickory leaves opened out. The last of the redbud blossoms were gone and the dogwoods were raining their petals down, and so were the fruit trees in the orchard.

The old tractor was crusted with a layer of wilted pink and white petals. Ted decided he'd better take a look at those screws. Some of them had loosened a bit under the vinegar treatment, and he worked on them for a while. He had a can of machine oil that he'd left there and he squirted it around the loosest of the screws and nuts and twisted again. Two of them actually came out, and he was so absorbed in his work he'd long since forgotten the barn and the twins, when a voice at his elbow said, "It's kind of sad, isn't it?"

He turned around and the twins, with their hands full of peanut butter cookies, stood gazing sorrowfully at the tractor.

"What d'you mean, sad?" he asked peevishly.

"Sad," repeated Bobbin. "Like a faithful old horse that's all broken down."

"It's like that poem about the ship," added Winkie. "You know, about 'Tear her tattered insides out.' "

"Have a cookie," said Bobbin, offering one.

"It's 'Tear her tattered ensign down,' " growled Ted. "You are an ignoramous." He took the cookie.

"Oh," said Winkie. "I thought it was 'insides out.' They were tearing her up, I thought, and it looked like the first thing to do was take out the insides."

"What's an ensign?" asked Bobbin.

"It's a flag," answered Ted and grinned a little. Maybe what Winkie had thought wasn't as dumb as what he had thought the first time he'd heard that poem. It was just after Steve's cousin Petey Hanson had become an ensign in the Navy. And the picture that had stuck in Ted's mind was of Petey dressed in a ragged patched uniform, standing in a sort of crow's-nest while people jumped and strained and stretched to grab hold of him and pull him down.

"We didn't know you'd come up here to work on your tractor," put in Bobbin suddenly. "We thought you'd come up to explore the barn."

Ted's thoughts moved very swiftly. Now that he was almost certain that the barn was the scene of some sort of mysterious goings on, it occurred to him that it probably wasn't such a good idea to have the twins poking around it. They might get hurt. They were certain to do something foolish. And anyway he wanted a chance to make a thorough investigation all by himself, to see if there really was some kind of mystery, before he told Daddy. Ted was nearly twelve years old, well, nearly eleven and a half, and he had enough sense to know that he couldn't handle spies or even car thieves all by himself. That is, he probably could, but it might be best to have a grown person around, just in case something came up that he couldn't cope with. Like guns.

So now he said, "For Pete's sake, that's baby stuff, all that about ghosts and spies and monsters. I'm tired of playing that baby game. Run along, I'm working."

"Game?" cried Bobbin indignantly. "We didn't make up anything. There really *were* all those things. And how about that light? You saw it yourself."

"Oh, you just saw shadows and things," said Ted. "And those lights were—were static electricity or something."

There was a pause. The twins looked at each other and then looked at Ted. And finally Winkie spoke. "Well, then," she said, "how about that black box in the barn? The one with all those wires?"

◆ Chapter Nine

Ted did his best not to appear startled. "Oh, that box," he said at last. "How'd you find it?"

"We saw it through a hole," answered Bobbin.

"This morning, before you came up," contributed Winkie.

"That box," repeated Ted slowly. "That—that's just a box to—to exterminate rats. That's it. Mother had it put in to exterminate rats."

"You use poison gas to exterminate rats," cried Bobbin. "You don't use a black box with wires sticking out from it. And it's dangerous. My Daddy told me if a dog smelled just a little whiff of that gas, he'd drop dead."

"Now look at that barn," said Ted scornfully. "How could you use poison gas in a barn like that? It's all full of cracks. The gas would go leaking out everywhere and kill all the dogs in the neighborhood—all the people too."

"And the cows," added Winkie. "And the birds and the butterflies and the earthworms and the . . ."

"Oh, shut up," said Ted. "Anyway, that's what that black box is. I expect Mother had it done and just forgot to say anything. I think maybe that's why the door's locked. Because maybe that box is dangerous to people, the way it is to rats, and the exterminators locked the doors to keep out children and dogs and things."

Bobbin turned and looked at the barn. Finally he walked up to it and followed along the rough siding till he came to a board with a large knothole in it. Then he stopped and peered in through the knothole, the center of which had fallen or been pushed out.

Ted wiped his hands on his blue jeans and went to stand beside him. Bobbin just went on looking intently through the hole. "Let me see," Ted said finally and Bobbin stood aside.

"You can't see it as well now as you could before," he explained. "The light showed all the wires good and plain this morning. But you can see the box, and I don't think it's exterminating anything. And I'm going to ask Aunt Priss."

Ted squinted through the hole. It was dim in the barn. An occasional ray of sunlight squeezed in through a crack in the boards. Dust motes drifted down the rays like specks of foam on a river.

And right there almost directly in front of the knothole was a black box. It was about a foot and a half square but only about half that high. Something that might have been a wire curled out of the side and something that might have been a knob sat on top.

Ted pressed his face up against the splintery boards and wondered how he'd gotten himself into this mess. If Bobbin asked Mother, she would call the police. Then Ted would never have a chance to do any investigating on his own, and the twins would have triumphed over him in a half dozen ways.

For it was the twins who had immediately spotted something mysterious going on, who had courageously gone to investigate in the dead of night, and who had not been bamboozled by any of the red herrings Ted had drawn across their path.

And that wasn't the way things were supposed to have worked out at all.

The curious box said "spies" as plain as day to Ted. It could be a shortwave radio type thing or something like a Geiger counter or—or anything spies used. It didn't look like monsters or ghosts or car thieves to him. And even though he didn't think he'd be able to capture a spy ring all by himself, Ted did long to get a look at just one of them, so he could identify the culprit for the police or the FBI or whoever came after spies.

And, of course, that was much too dangerous a thing for the twins to be involved in.

He was desperately trying to think of some way to mislead them effectively, when Bobbin cried, "Oh, boy, here comes Uncle Ralph!"

"Now we can go on the hike," added Winkie. And the two of them went dashing down the hillside shrieking, "The hike! The hike!"

Ted wondered if they really knew what a hike was.

The way they were hollering about it, they must think it was a three-layer chocolate cake.

He walked very slowly going home, and by the time he got there everybody was ready to leave, and his father had even found the canteen where Ted had left it in the linen closet. Ted was pleased to see that his mother had packed some fruit and cookies to take with them. He was beginning to regret having refused lunch. He helped himself to a banana right away on the grounds that if he didn't get his share early the twins would eat everything before he got around to it.

"Are we ready to leave?" asked Mrs. Garland. "Bobbin, do tie your shoes. This is rough walking and I don't like to see you tripping over your laces. Ted, get that package of Kleenex off the hall table and bring me some. Winkie keeps sneezing. And where are my binoculars?"

"Well, let's hurry up," cried Mr. Garland. "There're the glasses on the window sill. I've got the Kleenex, Ted. Make it snappy with those laces, Bobbin, and let's get started. I'm afraid it's going to rain before we get up there if we don't get a move on."

Ted expected lowering skies and thunder and lightning outside the way his father talked. Actually the sun could still be seen through a thin yellow haze, and the day was hot and strangely quiet. Every now and then a little wind picked up the dust in the road and whirled it around and then softly laid it down again. Only off to the west clouds towered up in an ominous gray tidal wave. But they didn't seem to be coming closer.

Still, it was going to storm, anybody could tell that.
Things were breathless and waiting the way it was
before a storm.

The walkers followed the track to the barn but left
it below the crest of the hill and went along under
the orchard wall. They passed the azalea patch and the
spring where the children had bound up their wounds
the day before. Ted glanced over his shoulder at the
barn. There it sat, hunched and comfortable among its
trees, as weathered and placid as a toad. Who would
dream the things that went on there—ghosts and
monsters were bad enough, but spies! It suddenly
seemed silly to Ted until he remembered all those
strange happenings and particularly that black box.

"Goodness, it really is hot," said Mrs. Garland,
using about a third of the Kleenex to wipe her face.
"It just doesn't seem like April at all."

"It'll be chilly again after it rains," said Mr. Garland. "And just be glad rain is all we're going to get.
There are tornado warnings out."

"Ralph!" cried Mrs. Garland.

"They're all a good bit west of here," said Mr.
Garland soothingly. "But we're bound to have a heavy
rain, and I did want to see if I couldn't find those
boundary markers this afternoon. So let's all have a
few drops of our precious water and then strike out
across the desert. Bobbin, mind your camels, they're
coming unlaced again."

Bobbin bent to tie his shoes and Mrs. Garland offered everybody an apple, and they went on.

In the woods it was spring again. The air became

cooler and fresher at once, especially down in the hollows where the little streams and springs bubbled along and the great trees stood up tall and silent around them. Some of the trees were so huge that Mr. Garland estimated they must have been good-sized trees in the days when Chief Five Owl had owned the farm.

Most of them were hemlocks, dark and weeping, with their drooping branches and their somber masses of needles. But some were beeches and these were the ones Ted liked, with their smooth warm gray bark and their twisting trunks. The children came on one beech which had fallen over during the winter. Its roots were still in the ground, however, and its branches bore as many tiny pale green leaves as if it were still upright. Bobbin put a hand on the great trunk.

"It's like a dinosaur," he said in an awed tone. "Like a big old dinosaur, fallen and dying."

Ted saw he was right. He could almost see the big trunk writhe and struggle to rise up out of the laurel bushes.

Among the tree's branches it was different. It was like being inside a green waterfall, with the tiny leaves spraying around them like drops of water. Ted and the twins twisted in and out, following each other along the limbs. And right by Ted's ear something went shooting out into the open and he recognized the high sweet whiffling sound of a dove's wings.

After a minute or two they found the dove's nest, a messy arrangement of about eight twigs with two white eggs in it, and Bobbin and Winkie got so excited they almost fell off the branch they were sitting on. Ted thought it was kind of exciting to find a bird's nest with eggs too. But already this spring he'd found a wren's nest on the back porch, a round bundle of dry grasses with a hole in the side through which he could just glimpse four tiny eggs with their million brown spots. And then he'd come on a robin's nest in a cedar tree, a mud-walled grass-lined cup, holding those gleaming blue eggs as carefully as a pair of gentle hands. It made the dove's foolish nest and plain white eggs seem, well, a little bit dull.

Ted's mother and father came to see the nest, but his mother took so long to get there, since she kept finding jack-in-the-pulpits, long curving sprays of blooming Solomon's-seal, and columbine and blue-bells, that they got tired of waiting for her and went on.

The twins were very interested in everything their Aunt Priss showed them—a silverbell tree with its thousands of big white blossoms dangling among the green leaves; or a redstart, flashing black and orange, tumbling down a tree trunk after a gnat, opening and closing its bright fanlike tail; or crossvine flowering high in the top of a pine tree. Ted kept hoping Bobbin and Winkie would drop back and stay with her, so he could walk with his father by himself.

His father could find plenty of good things on a hike, too, and he was willing to go the hard way around, up steep banks and down sheer rock slopes, and Ted liked that.

Though Winkie eventually went back to walk with

Mrs. Garland, Bobbin stuck like a burr. He followed
Ted and his father over the roughest parts of the trail
without any complaints. It was true the twins went
up and down pretty awkwardly, looking to be all
skinny knees and elbows, but they tackled anything
without hesitation. Ted couldn't help according them
a kind of grudging admiration. He still suspected it
might be just because they were too dumb to know
when to be scared. But even keeping on at that took a
certain amount of grit. He had to be fair about it.

It took a while to get to the property line and then
it took a longer while to find the iron stakes that
marked the exact spot. Mother and Winkie came
ambling along at last, and everybody had apples and
peanut butter cookies and the last of the water from
the canteen.

"What's the time?" asked Mrs. Garland. "I'd love
to walk back the long way round and show the twins
that waterfall and see if the saxifrage is blooming."

Mr. Garland considered. "You all go," he said at
last. "I think I'd better get back and start the fire in
the grill if we're going to have supper before it rains."

"I'll go," Ted volunteered. He hoped he sounded
noble and virtuous, but the truth was he'd never had a
chance to make the fire in the grill all by himself and
he was dying to try. And he didn't mind leaving the
twins behind either. Being by himself was getting to
be a rare thing these days and he was going to enjoy it.

His mother gave him that look which says quite
plainly, "I am trusting you to be careful and I am

showing how much I trust you by not saying it out loud," and Ted gave her that look that says, "For Pete's sake, do I look too dumb to be careful?" and his father told him where the lighter fluid was and they parted.

Ted followed a path that brought him out of the woods sooner than he had expected. He had thought it would lead back to the house, but of course there wasn't any real reason to suppose it would. He couldn't make out exactly where he was. The ground fell sharply away below him with big boulders scattered here and there. He scrambled down the slope and as he passed one boulder something caught his eye.

A snake lay along the top of the gray rock, carelessly curved and looped over the smooth surface. It was about three feet long, Ted estimated, gleaming blue-black and slender. He crept closer and when he was almost near enough to touch the creature, it raised its head and hissed warningly. Then it slid off across the rock and down the other side, moving in that marvelous way that snakes move, as smoothly and effortlessly as water flowing. Ted was delighted and went on down the rest of the way in a cheerful mood.

It didn't take him long to find the road to the house and he set off briskly. He wanted to have plenty of time to get the fire started all by himself. When he came in sight of the barn he stopped. He hadn't thought about spies or monsters or mysteries once since they'd passed the barn earlier. And even if he had thought, he hadn't had an opportunity to bring the subject up tactfully with his father, to find out without actually asking right out whether he thought spies were a thing you were likely to run across.

But the twins, he reflected gloomily, were now enjoying endless opportunities to talk about all the strange happenings and, worst of all, the black box.

He rounded a bend in the road and came smack on a man standing gazing up at the barn. The man was dressed in comfortable-looking outdoor sort of clothes and he was young and good-looking. One of the spies, thought Ted in some agitation. But would a spy really have such friendly blue eyes and such a pleasant crinkly grin?

"Hi," said the stranger.

"Hi," answered Ted cautiously. The young man put his hands in his pockets and took a couple of steps in the direction of the highway.

Then he stopped. He looked gravely at Ted a few minutes. "Do you believe in ghosts?" he asked finally.

"I—I don't think so," Ted stammered.

"Well," said the young man, "I didn't think I did either. But I just saw one. In that old barn."

And he strode off, leaving Ted standing there with his mouth hanging open.

✑ Chapter Ten

Ghosts again, thought Ted, as he sprinkled lighter fluid over the paper and kindling in the grill. Very, very carefully he struck a match and dropped it among the wads of paper. With a satisfying *hoosh!* flames shot up through the bars and then died away. Ted peered in anxiously. So far, so good. The sticks were beginning to catch.

Of course that man might just have been a plant. The spies could easily have arranged for one of the children to meet a pleasant-appearing young man on the road and have him mention ghosts, just to throw the children off the track.

But it didn't make much sense. Ted and the twins had gone to the barn in the dead of night once already to investigate ghosts and monsters. It was obvious they weren't scared of silly things like that. The young man would have done better to say he was an exterminator and tell Ted to keep away from the barn.

Ted poked at the fire and then glanced around at the barn. If it weren't for fear these old sticks would quit burning and make a mess of his fire, he'd just go up there this minute, without the twins or anybody, and make a real investigation. He'd find out what was actually going on, all by himself.

"Anyway, too late," he said aloud as he saw the others coming through the old orchard. But he wished he'd run after that young man and tried to find out more about the ghosts.

"Is the fire going well?" called his mother when they got closer. "Oh, good, I'm starving. Let's bestir ourselves and get things ready."

So they bestirred themselves, but all the same it was nearly an hour before they had found all the vital pickles and mustard and paper plates and gotten the hamburgers and rolls on the grill and made the twins wash their really filthy hands and faces.

Mother kept hurrying them along and, as she said, hurrying the twins just made things worse than ever. "It's like trying to hurry a drop of water," she said. "No matter how hard you try, it just goes where it wants to go and all you get is wet. And I'm sure we're all going to get wet before supper's over. *Look* at that sky."

The sky was certainly ominous, the clouds were low and thick and a curious kind of yellow-gray color Ted had never seen before. Once in a while a huge flash of lightning lit up behind them, but there was no thunder. It was still quite hot, and though you could sometimes see clouds scudding along overhead, there seemed to be no air at all moving down on the ground.

Ted remembered what his father had said about tornadoes, but he didn't mention it because he didn't want to scare the twins. Or Mother either. But he noticed that Daddy kept glancing up at the strangely threatening sky, and it seemed to Ted that he looked worried.

When the hamburgers were gone they roasted marshmallows over the coals. The twins toasted thousands. Ted ate only two. It was too hot to stand near the fire, and anyway toasted marshmallows weren't his top-favorite dessert. Besides, the hot night and the sinister sky and the stillness made everything seem all wrong. Toasting marshmallows was for fall evenings, brisk and dark and windy, noisy with crickets and the sound of dry leaves crackling.

"What we need now," said Mrs. Garland, "is Winkie's accordion. Then she could play one of her sad songs for us. Remember how she used to cry all the time she was playing? Even something like 'Little Brown Jug'?"

"I don't play the accordion anymore," said Winkie slowly. "Anyway I didn't cry because the songs were sad. I cried because when I squeezed the accordion it pinched my stomach."

Mrs. Garland laughed, but Winkie looked so pained that she stopped. "It wasn't funny," said Winkie. "It hurt."

"Well," said Mrs. Garland, "why didn't you stop playing or at least complain to your teacher?"

"I couldn't tell my teacher," exclaimed Winkie in a

scandalized voice. "He was a man. And anyway I thought everybody got their stomachs pinched. I just thought they were braver than I was."

Now both Mr. and Mrs. Garland laughed, and even Ted grinned. Winkie still looked a little injured, but then Mr. Garland gave her his marshmallow, which was done the way only he could do them, crisp golden brown all over, not scorched anywhere, and exactly right inside—gooey, but not absolutely melted. His father was the only person Ted knew who could toast a marshmallow perfectly every time. He said it was a gift, like perfect pitch, but Ted was inclined to think it was having arms long enough to stand away from the fire and take your time turning the stick without roasting yourself instead of the marshmallow. He could hardly wait to grow as tall as his father and have arms that long.

"Ted, you look kind of peaked," said his mother suddenly. "Do you think you're coming down with Steve's ailment?"

"I've had the mumps," answered Ted.

"Well, Steve didn't have mumps after all," said Mrs. Garland. "He had a virus or something. I talked to his mother this morning and she said the swelling and fever were all gone when he woke up today and she thought he might be able to come out for a while tomorrow."

"Oh, boy," said Ted dolefully. And after a while he got up and went to bed.

The twins went upstairs shortly afterward. They did

not go to bed. They sat on the edge of Winkie's bed, dressed in their white robes and pajamas. They did not speak, but each was quite well aware of what the other was thinking. It was not fair of Ted to say they were babies and couldn't tell shadows from something real. It was wrong to think they had imagined all those clues and lights and things. If they went to the barn now, this minute, they might see something or find something that would prove they were right. It was quite easy to climb out Winkie's window and over the roof of the front porch and down the trellis. Still without speaking, they rose and walked together to the window and Bobbin loosened the hook on the screen. . . .

Some way down the road from the barn a pleasant-looking young man, who owned a very delicate and valuable piece of equipment which he felt to be in danger, shut the door of his car, muttered to himself, and set off through the shadows. . . .

In his room Ted tossed and turned. Had the twins blabbed everything to Mother and Daddy? He figured probably not. Nobody had mentioned anything about the barn and its mysterious contents. The twins could only think about one topic at a time. On a walk in the woods, a walk in the woods would be the only thing their feeble brains could deal with.

At least he almost thought that was true.

But wouldn't the twins come to visit just as something really great happened! If he'd been by himself these last two days, or with Steve, by now he could have laid some kind of trap for the spies or ghosts or car thieves or whatever they were.

The twins would remember to ask Mother about the black box tomorrow, he knew that. Oh, darn!

Restlessly he climbed out of bed and looked out the window. The sky was still that menacing color, casting a weird glow over the landscape, so he could dimly make out things below. He looked toward the barn. Was that a light? Did he see something flash? Was it too early for lightning bugs? *And what was that white thing moving along the track?*

That settled it. He grabbed up his blue jeans and tennis shoes. He could sneak down the stairs and out through the kitchen and Mother and Daddy would never know, even though they were still sitting in the living room. . . .

Mr. Garland said to his wife, "I hear the wind rising. I must say this is funny weather. I mean funny-peculiar. It's a little worrisome."

He put down his book and got up and went out on the front porch. The sky was boiling with clouds, the wind roared up and then died quite suddenly, the air was leaden and warm. Things stirred fitfully here and there.

Was that flash a lightning bug? What was that light? Mr. Garland stared thoughtfully and went back in the house.

"Have the twins said anything else about ghosts?" he asked.

Mrs. Garland pondered. "I don't think so," she answered. "But they've all three spent a lot of time at the barn. Not inside. Just hanging around under that big oak."

"Hmm-mm," Mr. Garland said. "What'd I do with my flashlight?". . .

Bobbin and Winkie, clutching each other's hands, crept toward the barn. They went slowly. It was hard to see the path and the wind blew sudden gusts of warm gritty air around them. Once in a while there was again that odd behind-the-clouds glow of lightning, and now it was followed by faint thunder.

"Maybe we should have brought an umbrella," whispered Winkie.

"What?" whispered Bobbin. And then he stopped short. In the last flash of lightning he had distinctly seen somebody or something moving along the road. . . .

The young man reflected that he had been stupid to leave that box in the barn. He would be in deep trouble if anything happened to it. And now this weather wasn't going to help. Oh, well, he'd probably be able to protect himself and the box; he was equipped to do it. . . .

In the windy dark Ted climbed the slope toward the barn. He didn't take the track, he went around below the orchard and quietly climbed over the stone wall. He slipped behind his tractor and, going very cautiously, approached the barn. Was the door open tonight? He glanced in that direction. Was that a flowering bush of some sort, that big pale blob? He didn't remember anything like that so close to the barn. He watched and could make nothing of it. And then it seemed to him to move!

He couldn't help being scared. The thing was big and white and it didn't move like a person, it went forward slowly, slowly, in a sort of humping motion.

Maybe it was a cow. Sometimes somebody's cow strayed right into the Garlands' yard. But it didn't look much like a cow. It must be a bush. It wasn't really moving, the wind just made him think it was moving. . . .

In the next flash of lightning Mr. Garland looked up at the barn. That must be what he'd seen, that flash was a reflection of the lightning from some piece of metal on the roof or from one of the iron hinges on the big wooden shutters over the window in the loft.

Was there something white up there? A stray cow maybe? He'd better investigate. It wouldn't do to have a cow come tramping into the yard to eat the tulips and step on the iris. . . .

Lightning blazed above the clouds. The stray cow was suddenly very still. It had seen someone—just an ordinary human someone—moving toward it through the orchard. But coming from the other direction was that horrible shapeless greeping figure! The cow suddenly wished it had not come out alone. . . .

Mr. Garland did not see anything. He was staring up at the clouds and wondering if there really was going to be a tornado close by and whether he shouldn't go home rather than go rounding up stray cows. . . .

By this time Ted thought his imagination must be playing tricks on him. He seemed to be surrounded by stealthy figures. Anybody could be sneaking up behind him. He glanced over his shoulder. Surely there really was somebody coming up the hill.

He acted partly on impulse and partly on a feeling that having his back up against something would make him less jittery. He fled for the barn and through the door, which was now unlocked and standing wide-open. The barn was piled up with broken boxes and stacks of half-rotted lumber and various tall metal cans. None of it was really effective for hiding a good-sized eleven-year-old boy, but Ted crouched behind two of the cans and hoped he didn't stick out too much. He did have the wall at his back now, and it made him feel a little more secure until he thought about rats.

"There aren't any rats," he told himself firmly, and right then and there he forgot about them. For a curious dim light suddenly appeared in the barn door-way, and directly in front of him was the awful shapeless dreadful monster thing that Bobbin and Winkie and he had seen from Winkie's window!

⮂ Chapter Eleven

The thing was surrounded by a sort of dim glow. Ted thought that was the worst part. It stood for several minutes framed in the doorway. And then slowly it began to move—straight toward Ted! He knew it couldn't see him, or at least he didn't think it could. It came on, closer and closer, shining softly and horribly. Ted would have yelled, only he was so scared he couldn't get enough breath to yell. It was like one of those ghastly dreams in which you want terribly to move only you can't. For a minute he hoped it was a nightmare, but he knew darn well it wasn't.

The thing stopped. It stood quite still for a moment, and then it was suddenly transformed. All at once the hideous outer covering, whatever it was, fell away, and there stood the young man Ted had seen in the road that afternoon, holding a flashlight and gazing around the barn.

The young man flashed the light here and there. Outside, the wind and lightning and thunder increased. They were going to have a storm, and no mistake.

Mr. Garland prepared to turn back toward the house. But there *was* a light in the barn! He'd have to look into it. The white cow seemed to have disappeared.

The cow, as a matter of fact, having seen two figures or shapes or monsters or things go into the barn, had made up its two minds. It straightened up and became two small white-robed people and raced for the back of the barn. In a matter of seconds the twins had disappeared into the shed.

"Do you think we ought to go into the loft?" whispered Bobbin.

"We'd better," answered Winkie. "Something might come after us. Maybe we can hide up there. We can't hide here."

That was true, the shed was empty. Still holding Winkie's hand, Bobbin felt his way over to the ladder.

The wind roared, the sky was lit with streaks and flashes of lightning, rain spattered down in big heavy blobs. Mr. Garland, who had been approaching the barn very slowly and cautiously, suddenly began to run toward it.

In the barn the young man bent over his precious black box and started to detach some wires from it. The wind shook the old building and dust stirred and rose around Ted. He hoped he wasn't going to cough. All the boards creaked.

The strange man raised his head and looked up into the top of the barn. He picked up his flashlight and let the beam play here and there among the rafters. Suddenly he stood up and went over to the rough and broken steps leading up to the loft.

Cautiously Ted got to his feet. He knew what he meant to do. He'd grab that box and run out into the night. Whatever the spy was up to, Ted intended to see he didn't get away with it.

There was a sudden terrible scream from the loft and another and another. Ted jumped half out of his skin. Nothing human made that noise!

A rushing scurrying noise sounded overhead and the spy, halfway up the stair, cried, "Yee-ow! Help!" and the light of his flashlight showed two dim white figures at the top of the steps, two small colorless ghostly forms, and then all at once over their heads two more white things, big-headed and screaming and flapping and growling.

Ted was not so scared that he forgot the black box. He dashed forward to get it, but without light he couldn't locate it. The shrieking was still going on and the wind and the thunder and then all at once a voice, a deep and familiar one, cried, "What's going on here?" and the stranger fell off the steps.

He got up, coming straight for Ted, who had just located the black box. "You get away from that, you idiot!" he cried, and Ted tumbled over backward and the twins half fell, half slid down the steps and the wind's roar rose higher and the young man cried, "Run! We've got to get out of here!"

Winkie picked a jonquil up out of the mud and looked at it sadly. "Poor thing," she mourned. "It's all dirty and torn up. They all are."

"They look just the way you all did last night when you came in," said Mrs. Garland. "But we won't worry too much about it. The tulips and iris are coming along beautifully. And maybe next year the jonquils will have a better chance. That's the really wonderful thing about a garden, no matter what happens this year, you've always got next year to look forward to."

"That was some storm," commented Ted. "Here's a piece of the barn roof." And he poked at it with his foot. They all glanced up at the barn. Some of the roof was missing. Last night Ted had expected much worse. When the stranger had yelled for them to run, the first thing that had popped into Ted's head was "Bomb!" He just knew that black box was a bomb and they were all going to be blown to bits and he hadn't waited a minute. He'd fled out into the lashing rain and the wind, a howling fury pushing and shoving against him. He could still remember quite plainly how scared and confused he'd been, and how everybody seemed to be yelling and screaming and running.

"Here comes the spy," said Winkie now, but Ted squinted down the road at the approaching car and said happily, "No, it's Steve. He must be all right."

Steve's mother let him out where the track divided to go to the barn and then she turned around and went bouncing off. She was always in a hurry. Ted and the twins went to meet Steve.

Steve was done up in sweaters and scarfs. It was chilly this morning, almost cold, and evidently Steve's mother thought he was still delicate. At any rate he was all bundled up.

"Hi," he said to the twins, but when he saw Ted he was speechless. "What happened to you?" he asked finally. "You look like you'd been bear fighting."

Ted grinned. He knew he was a really alarming sight. He wouldn't have supposed that simply falling over all that junk in the barn could bang him up so thoroughly. One of his eyes was black, his face and arms were covered with scratches and bruises, and he had a gash on his chin.

"A ghost did it," explained Winkie and giggled.

"A monster," added Bobbin.

"Car thieves, bank robbers, spies," cried Winkie, and she and Bobbin leaned on each other's shoulders and laughed helplessly.

Ted looked at them for a minute and then he grinned again. After all, it was the only thing to do, laugh, that is.

"What's going on?" asked Steve. "What's so funny?"

And right at that moment it all struck Ted as very funny indeed, especially last night with all of them creeping around in the dark scaring each other to death, and he laughed till he had to sit down on the grass. His mother yelled at him to get up, the ground was soaking wet.

"What's the matter?" asked Steve crossly. "If you don't quit laughing and tell me, I'm going home."

So Winkie told him, all about everything, the mysterious lights and the "greeping" figure, the padlock on the door, the black box, the clues, including the apples. It all sounded pretty silly. Ted couldn't help being a little ashamed of himself.

But Steve didn't seem to think it was silly. "Gee,

neat-o," he said. "But what was it? I know it wasn't ghosts. Was it really bank robbers?"

"Spies," chortled Bobbin. "It was spies." And he and Winkie began to laugh again.

In the end Ted had to do the explaining. "It was this man named Dick Sutton," he said. "He's a real great guy. He works for the telephone company in the afternoons and evenings. But in the morning he goes to school to learn about nature and biology and things like that. He's getting some kind of thing, what was it? Oh, a master degree or something."

"Well, what was he doing?" persisted Steve. "Why was he hanging around your barn."

"He was taking pictures," said Ted and stopped. He liked to think he'd known all along that blinding silent blue-white flash was a photographic flash bulb. After all, he was a newspaperman's son, and he'd seen pictures taken with a flash about a billion times.

But somehow it was so unexpected in a barn in the middle of the night, and he knew in his most inside heart that he hadn't recognized it for what it was.

Steve opened his mouth to complain again, and Ted hurried on. "He was studying owls, mostly; barn owls live in our barn. But he wanted to see all about what kind of things live in a barn with barn owls, so he set up cameras to take pictures of what went in and out. And he put apples and corn and seeds around as bait to make the animals come to get their pictures taken. That's what all the flashing was. He couldn't stay out here much, the way he wanted to, because of going to school and working. So he used photographs of what went on when he wasn't there to sort of tell him what happened."

Steve looked puzzled. "How do you take pictures if you're not there?" he queried.

"Well, you just get the camera arranged so it's all ready to go off," explained Ted. "So just the least little thing will make the shutter flip or whatever it does. And you attach a real fine wire or some nylon thread or something to the camera, to the little trigger-thing that makes it work, and if an animal touches the wire, the camera right away takes its picture. At least it's supposed to, but Mr. Sutton says it doesn't work very well. He thinks a movie camera would do better. But you can see how it ought to work. You could put one of those wires across the steps to the loft, for instance, and if a 'coon went up, then you'd know some 'coons had been in the barn and that some of them didn't mind about owls being around and might even try to go up in the loft with them. And that's the kind of thing Mr. Sutton is trying to find out."

"Gee," said Steve. "But what about the black box? What did it have to do with owls?"

"It counts owls, I think," said Ted. "I don't know how it works, but what it does is make a record of how many times the owls light to feed their little ones. It works sort of like that thing that counts cars on the highway, you know, when you run over that sort of rope and there always is a black thing sitting in the

weeds by the roadside? But this had to work on owls
and it was a lot more complicated than those highway
things."

"It was his own invention," said Winkie rather
proudly.

"It has electronic tubes in it," Bobbin added im-
pressively. "And some of them weren't his. And that
was why he came out here last night, because the
weather worried him and he wanted to bring the box
back to his house."

"But the barn didn't blow away, like we thought it
would when that wind came roaring up and he hol-
lered for us to run," Ted went on. "At least the others
thought the barn was going to blow down. I thought
it was going to blow up."

"And Mr. Sutton wanted us to run to his car, and
Uncle Ralph wanted us to run to the house," cried
Bobbin. He and Winkie began to pull and tug at each
other, just as the two men had hauled them back and
forth last night. "And Mr. Sutton pulled and Uncle
Ralph pulled and everybody yelled," Winkie shouted,
and the twins danced around each other, shoving and
tusseling. "And it was just like the Lobster Quadrille
in *Alice*," Bobbin ended, and they both stopped dead
still. "Except it was raining," said Winkie solemnly.

Steve laughed. "You're nuts," he said. "But why
didn't he want to go to your house? Did he think it
might get blown away too?"

"Because he didn't know we were living there," said
Ted. "He just came around late at night and went to

the barn and he thought the house was still empty."

And that was the whole thing. If Mr. Sutton had known the Garlands had bought the farm, he would have come and told what he was up to and none of the mystery would ever have happened. They would have known what the wires and the lights were about, they would have realized that mysterious chart was just Mr. Sutton's reminder to himself of where he'd left the cameras in relation to the nest and the barn door, that "mi" and "grshpr" and "nstlg" stood for "mice" and "grasshopper" and "nestling," creatures the owls had fed to their young ones.

It had all turned out to be so mild and ordinary, it was a little bit disappointing. But Steve said, "Rats! A mystery! And I had to be sick and miss it."

"Not much of a mystery," Ted answered.

"Yes, it was," Steve insisted. "A mystery with clues and everything. And it got solved, too. Gee, I think it was neat. I think it was great the way you all got up and chased each other in the night." He paused a minute. "It was pretty brave," he added.

Ted didn't say anything. He planned never to let the twins know that he had thought the clues were his father's handiwork and he hadn't had to be brave to go running around in the dark. Except right there at the last when he did try to capture the black box, he hadn't actually been anywhere near as brave as the twins had been.

"Here comes the spy now," Winkie pointed out as

Mr. Sutton drove up in his dilapidated car. He smiled and waved at them and called out, "I've got something to show you."

They crowded around him when he got out of the car, and Steve was introduced. Mr. Sutton took something out of his pocket and held it up. It was a picture of someone or something, a thin white wispy featureless figure against a dark background. It certainly looked like a small ghost.

"It's me," said Bobbin in awed tones. "The night I ran into the barn."

Mr. Sutton nodded. "But do you wonder I thought the place was haunted?" he asked. "And last night when the owls screamed and I looked up in the loft and saw *two* of you, I nearly fainted. Gosh, you really had me going last night, scaring me to death and trying to steal my box and then not even letting me rescue you from the storm."

"Well, you had us going," confessed Ted. "The awful things we thought about you."

"I want to see the owls," said Bobbin. And Mr. Sutton agreed.

When they had assembled in the barn, Mr. Sutton picked up what he called his "monster clothes," another one of his inventions. It was a sort of pop tent, like a huge umbrella, really, without a handle. Mr. Sutton balanced it on his head and looked through a slit in the front and he became a curious shapeless awful headless monster creeping along.

"I wore this last night to keep off the rain, because I planned to carry my black box back to the car," he told the children.

"Don't you have a raincoat?" asked Winkie.

"Not with me," he answered. "But I always take this in my car when I'm owl-hunting. When I come and go this way, it doesn't seem to bother the owls as much as when I just walk in looking like a man," explained Mr. Sutton. "I'd turn my flashlight on underneath the tent so I could see, and if I went very slowly even the raccoons I found in here one night didn't notice me."

He chuckled. "But you know, once I did happen to think that if anybody saw me sneaking around in it, they'd certainly send for the police."

"Aunt Priss would have sent for the exterminators," said Bobbin gravely and looked surprised when Ted and Mr. Sutton both burst out laughing.

They all climbed the steps to the loft, going very quietly as Mr. Sutton told them to. When they were all crouching together in the dimness under the sloping roof, Mr. Sutton turned on a flashlight. Winkie gasped.

There in the strong beam were the curious monkey faces of two adult owls and three downy white young ones. They stared into the light, blinking their dark eyes and turning their heads a little from side to side.

After a bit Mr. Sutton turned off the flash. One of the owls screamed, that inhuman shriek which had terrified all of them, except Mr. Sutton, last night when the twins went up to the loft to escape the spy.

"Oh, goodness," gasped Winkie, and once more she half fell down the loft stairway.

"They're interesting," she said when they were all back on the barn floor. "But I don't like to hear them."

"They can be noisy," Mr. Sutton agreed. "And pretty fierce when they've got young ones. But I like owls best of almost all the birds."

"And you know what?" asked Bobbin suddenly. "Now this really is Five Owl Farm!"

·ℰ Chapter Twelve

"All set?" asked Mr. Garland.

"I think so," Winkie answered. She looked worried. "Aunt Priss, will you take a picture of Freddy's grave and send it to us?"

"Yes, I will," Mrs. Garland answered. "But we want you to come back this summer and spend some time with us, and you can see it then."

"Oh, we want to come, lots," Winkie assured her.

Ted groaned and slapped his forehead. "No, no, no!" he cried. "I can't bear it. Don't ruin my summer vacation too."

"Ted!" reproved his mother.

"It's all right, Aunt Priss," Bobbin said quickly. "He doesn't mean it. If he'd really meant it, he wouldn't have said it out loud; he'd have just thought it."

"A friendly insult, in other words," put in Mr. Garland. "Bobbin, I trust you have the tickets."

Bobbin nodded. "Yes, I do. I was careful with them."

"Well, where are they?" asked Mrs. Garland anxiously.

"In my big flashlight," said Bobbin.

By this time Ted felt he was an old hand at dealing with the twins. You didn't get impatient or try to hurry them; you just persisted and persisted till you got their whole attention and found out what you wanted to know.

"Where's the flashlight?" he asked briskly.

"It needs new batteries," explained Bobbin.

"Where is it?" Ted asked again.

"In the suitcase," said Winkie.

So while Mr. Garland muttered about missing the bus and Mrs. Garland shook her head over the state of the suitcase, everything jammed in any old way, Ted searched out the flashlight and unscrewed the end and peeled the bus tickets from around the batteries.

There wasn't any use asking the twins how they had thought the bus driver was going to collect the tickets from that particular place.

"We'll have to hurry," said Mr. Garland, and somehow he managed to get the twins to do it. Almost right away they were driving along the highway.

"I hope you've enjoyed your stay with us," Mr. Garland said, looking into the rearview mirror at the twins, side by side on the back seat.

"Yes," said Winkie primly. "It was very educational."

"It was?" asked Mr. Garland in some surprise. "What did you learn?"

There was a very long silence and finally Bobbin said, "We learned that those lizards with blue tails are really skinks."

That was one of the things Dick Sutton had told them. Gosh, Ted did hope that being with Mr. Sutton wasn't going to be educational; it might take all the fun out of it. Mr. Sutton was really great. He had explained how a phone worked so that Ted was almost certain he understood it.

He had taken Ted and Steve and the twins to the powerhouse to see the swallows migrating through, sitting black and hunched on the power lines by the thousand, and then suddenly filling the air with their lovely graceful flight, the blue and green flash of their backs and the swift liquid motion of their wings, sailing and darting and diving and swooping, until Ted was dizzy with watching.

He had taken them on a trip up the river in his motorboat, a good fast wet ride that Ted thought was close to being the most exciting thing he'd ever done. And he'd promised to take Steve and Ted again and teach them how to run the boat.

And maybe that would be educational. It was hard to tell, like the things Mr. Sutton had told them about cotton rats and voles and different kinds of mice that he said were what owls mostly ate. It had just seemed interesting at the time.

"Is that all?" asked Mr. Garland. "Didn't you learn anything else?"

"Yes," said Winkie. "I learned something. I left a gumdrop on the window sill and it got rained on and now it isn't any good at all. I didn't know gumdrops would melt."

Daddy laughed and Ted grinned. He might have known that whatever Winkie learned would be something unexpected. As a matter of fact, Ted thought, the twins were pretty educational themselves. He remembered how he'd felt about them when they first came, how he'd thought they were dumb and dopey and everything.

But they weren't so dumb and dopey. They were just different. They weren't ever going to be able to hit a ball hard and straight the way he and Steve could, well, the way he and Steve could once in a while. But they were all right, just the same.

That's what Daddy was always telling him, wasn't it? "Don't think people have to be just like you and do the things that you do and like the things that you like. People can have wings and a tail and purple spots and still they can be good people and pleasant people and people you can enjoy."

Ted hadn't known quite what he meant before, but now he did. In spite of everything, he'd gotten to know the twins well and to admire them in a way and even like and enjoy their nuttiness.

After all, this vacation would have been a lot duller if it hadn't been for Bobbin and Winkie and their lively imaginations and the crazy things they thought up to do and the venturesome way they went about doing them. He was glad they'd come.

"Bobbin, did you remember to wind your watch?" asked Mr. Garland.

"Yes, I did, Uncle Ralph," Bobbin answered. "But

don't call me Bobbin any more. I'm too old for that. Call me Bob, the way Mr. Sutton does."

"Sure thing," answered Mr. Garland. "And how about you, Winkie? Are you going to change your name?"

"And be Cynthia?" asked Winkie in horror. "That awful name? I guess I'll just be Winkie till I'm ninety and nine."

"I expect you will." said her uncle, smiling. "Look,

there's the bus station and there's your bus about to pull out."

They made it, but just barely. The twins had so little time to get aboard they hardly had time to lose anything.

"Someday," Mr. Garland said meditatively as he and Ted walked back to the car, "someday the twins are going to grow up and be recognizable human beings."

Ted grinned. "Maybe so," he answered. "But I hope they don't do it before this summer. I'm kind of looking forward to having the same old twins come back. What do you suppose they'll manage next time?"

"Goodness knows," said his father, and they got in the car and drove off.

ABOUT THE AUTHOR

Wilson Gage is the pen name of Mary Q. Steele, member of a gifted and successful family of writers; her husband, William, her sister, and her mother, Christine Govan, are the authors of many popular books for children and young people. Her first book *Secret of the Indian Mound* quickly established her in the children's-book field. All her books are characterized by her long interest in nature and regional history. In 1960 her book *The Secret of Fiery Gorge* was chosen as an Honor Book in the Children's Spring Book Festival of the New York *Herald Tribune*, and, more recently, *Big Blue Island* received the 1966 Aurianne Award of the Children's Services Division of the American Library Association.

Wilson Gage was born in Chattanooga, Tennessee, and is a graduate of the University of Chattanooga. She lives with her husband and three children in Signal Mountain, Tennessee.

ABOUT THE ARTIST

Paul Galdone is a free-lance artist with many books to his credit, among them *Miss Osborne-the-Mop* by Wilson Gage, published in 1963. Mr. Galdone lives in Rockland County, New York, with his wife and two children.